Time Sweep

VALERIE WELDRICK

Time Sweep

Illustrated by Ron Brooks

LOTHROP, LEE & SHEPARD COMPANY
A Division of William Morrow & Company, Inc.
New York

Printed in the United States of America.
First Edition
1 2 3 4 5 6 7 8 9 10

Library of Congress Cataloging in Publication Data
Weldrick, Valerie.
  Time sweep.

  SUMMARY: A boy is mysteriously transported from present-day Sydney, Australia, to the London of 1862.
  [1. Space and time—Fiction. 2. England—Fiction] I. Brooks, Ron. II. Title.
PZ7.W4493Ti   [Fic]   78-11837
      ISBN 0-688-41869-4   ISBN 0-688-51869-9 lib. bdg.

DUNBAR BRANCH

To my parents

1

It's not easy to begin living in a new place. Laurie was finding that out. What made it worse was the fact that he'd arrived in Sydney at the end of November, with so few weeks of the school year left that there'd been no point in starting, and while this made for a nice long holiday, it left him without the immediate circle of acquaintances that school would have brought. So, although he was good at amusing himself, there were times when he would have given a great deal to have someone to talk to, to plan some enterprise with, just to walk around with. One of these times occurred in the public library not long after the move. Forgetting where he was for the moment, he leaned his head on the books and kicked moodily at the bottom shelf. He told himself he was full of gloom, and was suddenly struck by the splendid qualities of the word. GLOOM. He hadn't thought of it before. Books that

spoke of "an aura of gloom" spoke nothing but the truth, because he felt certain a sort of personal fog, about two feet wide, hung about him wherever he went, muffling the sounds and dimming the sights of that other, happy world outside. He wondered whether the cloud was visible to others. Well, not *any* others, obviously, but special, sensitive people who . . .

". . . get into trouble," penetrated through the fog.

"What?" he said stupidly.

"I said, that librarian is watching you kicking the shelves, and if you don't stop you're likely to get into trouble," repeated a purposeful, dark-haired girl who'd appeared from goodness knows where.

"Oh." Jolted out of his private thoughts, Laurie continued to look at her vaguely.

"Besides, I want to get where you are. Are there any Rosemary Sutcliffs in?"

Now he was with her. "Do you read Rosemary Sutcliff?" he asked quickly.

"Why do you think I'm looking?" she replied severely.

Laurie spun around to face the shelves. "Have you read *Eagle of the Ninth*?" he asked eagerly.

"It's my favorite," she answered simply.

"Mine too."

They eyed each other, and the girl bit one dark plait speculatively.

"I've seen you about lately. Where do you live?" she asked finally.

9

"Brunswick Street."

"I thought so. The old Bailey place?"

"If that's number 44, yes. We've just moved from Melbourne."

"I live in 32."

"Oh, quite close."

"Yes."

Neither seemed to have anything more to say.

"Well, I'd better be going."

"What about Rosemary Sutcliff?"

"I've read those. I'm taking *A Traveller in Time*."

"Oh, that's very good."

"I know. I've read it before. Twice."

"So have I. My father says Mary Queen of Scots wasn't all she was cracked up to be."

"Does he? I don't know about that. I like the book anyway. I'll try Rosemary Sutcliff again tomorrow."

"Are you coming tomorrow?"

"Yes. Are you?"

"I come most days."

Laurie felt almost sure he wanted to ask the girl to go to the library with him. Almost sure. He wasn't used to girls—hadn't even thought about them much— but this one seemed to read. She might not want to go to the library with him, of course. He felt undecided, a bit shy and helpless.

"I'll call for you. What time?" said this very decided person.

"Would eleven o'clock do?" Laurie asked.

"Fine. See you."

"See you."

She turned to go, then appeared to think of something.

"I suppose your father doesn't like tall women. Mary Queen of Scots was nearly six feet, you know."

"Was she? I don't think her height comes into it."

"It probably does. Men don't like giant women," she insisted darkly, and left.

Laurie watched her to the door and then turned back to the shelves quite cheerfully. The fog had dispersed. He was part of the world again.

"Decided to give up attacking the furniture, have you?" asked a facetious young library assistant a little later, finding him bent quietly over a book.

"Yes, thank you," said Laurie dreamily, automatically polite. Then, realizing his opportunity, added, "Could you tell me what book I'd find the height of Mary Queen of Scots in, please?"

When he got home he dumped his books on the divan, careful not to disturb Rosie, the cat, whose nerves were bad since the move, chose the three biggest apricots from a bowl on the sideboard, and headed upstairs, where he could hear a lot of banging and scraping going on. It came not from the next floor but from the attic at the top of the house. Laurie

11

thought of this room with satisfaction, for it was to be his. It was tiny, with a sloping roof and a casement-covered window, and Laurie had a special, excited feeling about it because all his life till now had been lived at ground level.

He found his parents just completing the assembly of a bed that had certainly seen better days. It was brass, rather tarnished, and inset on each of five posts (three at the top and two at the bottom) were three marbly balls, rich blue on the bottom, reddy brown in the middle and speckled white on top.

"Oh, here you are, before your surprise is ready. Do you like it?" asked his mother proudly.

"It's mine, is it? It sags a bit."

"Oh, darling, we'll fix that," said his mother disappointedly.

"I'll lay a board right across the frame, I think, and we'll put the mattress on that," said his father, who wasn't really handy, but liked to think he was.

"Where did it come from?"

"A shop in Willoughby. We couldn't resist it. It's very old."

"It looks it."

"Oh dear, I do believe he'd be happier with some chrome and vinyl horror," said his mother, looking appealingly toward her husband.

"No I wouldn't, Mum, honestly," said Laurie quickly, sensing that he wasn't rising to the occasion. "I'm just getting used to it. I've never seen a bed like

12

it, that's all." Then, thinking what else he could say to give satisfaction, added, "I like those ball things. The colors are nice."

"That blue is called lapis lazuli, after the stone, Laurie," said his father. "If you can remember that tomorrow, I'll teach you to stand on your head. Got it? LAPIS LAZULI."

This was a serious offer, seriously received by Laurie.

"There's a maker's name here," said Mrs. Langridge, half under the bed. "It says, what is it, 'Jos.' I think, 'Jos. R. Jagger, St. Mary Axe, London.'"

"When would Jos. have made it?" asked Laurie.

"That's short for Joseph, Laurie," said his father, who never missed an opportunity to instruct. "Although I don't know. Joshua, perhaps."

"Or Josiah. But when did he make it? And why did he make it in church?" continued Laurie.

"It's high Victorian, wouldn't you say, dear?" said Mr. Langridge.

"Oh, certainly," replied his wife. "I'll be able to clean this tarnish away."

"Around 1850-60, I'd say," said Mr. Langridge, before Laurie could ask his question yet again. "And I'm sure he didn't make it in church. I imagine St. Mary Axe is or was a church that gave its name to a street."

"I wonder how and when it came to Australia," mused Laurie.

"One wonders, naturally, but I don't suppose we'll ever know," said his mother. "That's part of the charm of old things, don't you think? Now, it must be lunchtime. Is anyone hungry?"

"Just a little. It's nearly three o'clock," said Laurie. "Never!"

"It is, though. Why do you think I'm eating apricots? I don't like apricots."

"My goodness. I didn't realize, did you, Hugh?"

"Not for a moment."

"It was your not coming home that did it. Where have you been all this time?"

"The library."

"All the time?"

"No."

"Well then?"

"Oh, just around."

"Did you meet anyone 'around'?" asked his mother who, though not very observant, was becoming conscious of, and a little anxious about, her son's solitary ways.

"I met someone at the library, actually."

Mrs. Langridge brightened. "Someone interesting?"

"I'm not sure. It's a girl."

"That's not so frightful, is it?"

"Could be. I never knew a girl before."

"They're human beings, darling."

"She reads, anyway."

"That's nice. What's her name?"

14

Laurie, leading the procession down the stairs, paused.

"I don't know."

"What?"

"She didn't say."

"You didn't ask?"

"I was so surprised about Mary Queen of Scots, I suppose."

"Who?"

"And then, the librarian was looking at me so suspiciously."

"Why?"

"I'll see her tomorrow, anyway," concluded Laurie, and suddenly hurried off, remembering the books waiting for him beside Rosie.

"Do you suppose he's making her up?" asked Mrs. Langridge, clutching her husband's sleeve.

"If he were going to make anyone up, he'd make up a boy."

"I don't know. He's never been the same since the measles."

"Don't fret. We'll know soon enough."

✦

Laurie needed time to get used to new things, like Rosie, who still hadn't got used to being removed from the home of her kittenhood. By nighttime he was devoted to his new bed, had spent an hour polish-

15

ing it, and had discovered how infinitely satisfying it was to hold or rub the smooth, egglike knobs. He wanted to sleep in it. His parents discussed his request seriously. They never said he couldn't do things "because." Sometimes, contrarily, Laurie wished they wouldn't always be so very reasonable and solemn. Anyway, there was no refusal this time. One night on sagging springs wasn't going to give him curvature of the spine, said his father, and his mother was so reassured by his growing enthusiasm for her find that she was disposed to indulge him.

It was a humid, airless night, after a hot day. Clouds had built up in the late afternoon, and people had waited for the relief of a southerly, but when it came it wasn't very successful, lowering the temperature only slightly and blowing itself out fitfully a few hours later. Laurie woke up in the early hours of the morning with a great longing for ice water. What should he do? The nearest water was on the floor below, in the bathroom. He could creep there without disturbing his parents, he supposed; but what he really wanted was water from the refrigerator in the kitchen. Could he negotiate that far in the dark? In Melbourne he could flit around with great ease. That was a smaller house, of course, and all on one level, and most important of all, he was used to it. There were lots of hazards here—stairs, some of them creaky, turnings, the mess from the unpacking. He'd best put it out of his mind. Yet the more he tried to do that, the more

17

he wanted a drink. It would be so simple to take water to bed every night, said one interior voice, and another answered, why bother, when you hardly ever want it? But I want it *now*, insisted the first voice.

In the end, there was nothing to do but to obey the demands of the thirsty voice. He got up silently and padded to the door. The worst of it was that he'd never even slept in this room before—he could easily have gone to the kitchen from the living-room divan he'd shared with Rosie till now. Oh, for a mother who didn't think you'd come down with the plague the moment she heard a sound in the night. Did the woman never sleep?

He crept down the side of the stairs rather than the center, since he'd heard somewhere that that was the technique favored by burglars, and made his way to the kitchen without mishap. There was no stir from his parents' room. The refrigerator door slipped open with cooperative quietness and there was the water, silvery, icy, delicious. He drank it straight from the jug, and was glad he'd come. He didn't feel like the same person as that poor creature who'd tossed hotly in bed, lusting after water. When he'd drunk his fill he wiped his mouth on his arm, stroked Rosie, who'd miraculously appeared at his side the moment she heard the refrigerator door, and commenced the return journey. This, too, was accomplished safely, and he congratulated himself on his cleverness as he groped around the side of the bed and eased himself back in.

There seemed to be some sort of obstruction to the top sheet, though; somehow it had become caught on one side. Laurie tugged at it and froze as something rolled toward him. After a split second of frightened paralysis, he hit out with his hands, and kicked with his feet. He couldn't even think what he was lashing out at. He knew it wasn't Rosie, but in the idiocy of panic he kept thinking of a big dog. Actually, it was a person, as he realized when a voice suddenly cried out of the darkness, "Stop it, won't you? I didn't mean any harm, honest!"

Laurie sprang out of bed, very fuddled in the head but with enough sense left to take in the frightened note in the voice and to realize that, whatever was happening, there didn't appear to be any immediate danger to himself.

"Who are you?" he demanded, peering into the darkness and hoping he sounded fierce and unafraid.

"Frank Kilderbee, sir," replied the voice, as its owner extricated himself from the severely mauled sheets and stood up. Laurie could make out that it was a boy, about his own height, and fully dressed.

"What are you doing in my bed?"

"I'm sorry, sir. I heard as you was in Devon."

"Devon?"

"On account of your croup."

"Croup?"

"Or some such. I was that starved with the cold I *had* to take a chance the servants wouldn't catch me."

"Servants?"

19

"I'm sorry you're deaf, sir."

"I'm not the least bit deaf. It's just that you keep saying very peculiar things."

"I can't help it if I've never been to school," said the boy, firing up immediately.

"School has nothing to do with it. Let me get this straight," said Laurie, reaching for his bathrobe, and failing to find it. "You've mistaken me for someone else, obviously. Someone who's abroad."

"Abroad?"

"For his—what is it?—croup? Now . . . wait a bit," said Laurie, suddenly sidetracked. "If you've never been to school, why haven't the welfare people been on to you?"

"Welfare?"

"Now *you're* doing it. Look, why don't you just start at the beginning."

"Well, sir, it's just I was so cold, and so tired, and hearing the maid tell the cat's meatman that the family was gone, I climbed in through a back window and come upstairs while the servants was having their tea. I hid till they was all abed and then I come in here and got in that bed. I never been in a bed like it, neether."

"Weren't you taking a terrible risk?"

"I was and all, but just now I'd risk my head for a bed indoors."

"In *December*?" asked Laurie in surprise.

"*Especially* December," replied the boy, equally uncomprehending.

"Well, those southerlies do make a difference at that," said Laurie. "I'm getting quite cold myself. I can't think where my bathrobe's gone. But let's see . . . what shall I do with you?"

"Not the police, sir, please. I meant no harm," implored the boy.

Laurie rubbed his forehead worriedly. This was all so odd. Why did the boy keep calling him "sir"? And why was he so cold? Melbourne wasn't like this, summer *or* winter.

"If this is a sample, I don't think much of Sydney summers," he burst out fretfully.

"Sidney Summers, sir?" repeated the boy, just as nonplussed as Laurie by the strange turns the conversation kept taking.

"*Sydney summers*, for goodness' sake! And stop calling me 'sir.' "

"Sorry, Master Pemberton."

"That's not my name either."

"Then I'm sorry, I don't know who you are."

"I'm Laurie Langridge."

"You're staying here while the Pembertons are away?"

"We live here. We've just moved in."

"You live *with* the Pembertons?"

"I've never heard of the Pembertons! *We* live here. You're in the wrong house."

"This *is* number 16, isn't it?"

"44."

"Go on, you're pulling my leg."

"I tell you it's number 44. 44 Brunswick Street."

"16 Cavendish Square."

"Are you mad? I ought to know."

"So you ought, if you live here."

"You think I don't?"

"No more nor I do."

"Well, we can settle that easily enough. Come here."

They moved to the window and drew the curtains aside. It was freezing.

"There you are, see," crowed the boy.

Laurie was silent, severely rattled. It was dark outside, but something was very wrong. He felt a shiver up his spine that was only partly the cold. Trying desperately to pierce the blackness with his eyes, he thought he could make out much more open space than there ought to be; and surely there were bare-branched skeletons of trees in the middle of the road? And, silhouetted against the gray-black sky, chimney pots, lots and lots of them?

He gripped the window ledge tightly, feeling giddy.

"Just tell me one thing," he said grimly. "Where are we?"

"Cavendish Square. I'm right, see."

"But *where's* Cavendish Square?"

"What?"

"What city are we in?"

The boy stared at him. "Why, London."

Laurie's head reeled. He had been terribly afraid

the answer would be something like that. Of course, he could be dreaming. He closed his eyes to shut the strange scene out, and tried to think. *Had* he been awake when he got, or thought he got, the water? Water! He couldn't imagine wanting water. Hot tea, maybe. Perhaps he'd dreamed the heat. Or was he dreaming the cold? Yes, he was dreaming the cold, because it *was* December, even the boy agreed on that. And now, when he opened his eyes, it would all be gone, and he'd be back in his bed, and it would be morning, and he did remember lapis lazuli, so his father would teach him to stand on his head. He would show the girl and she'd be impressed—unless, of course, she could already stand on her head. He opened his eyes hopefully, and there was the gray-black scene. Solid, terraced houses across the square; bare trees. Other things, too, that frightened him more. An absence of cars. No television antennae. No telephone poles. Street lamps—yes, lamps.

"What year is it?" he asked, looking straight ahead, trying not to feel anything.

"Year? It's 1862, everyone knows that. By jingo, no wonder they wanted to get you away to Devon. I reckon putting it about that you had the croup was just a tale. Croup! More like it's brain fever."

1862. 1862. 1862. Don't panic, don't panic, thought Laurie, and fell down in a faint.

When he came to, the strange boy was trying to heave him into bed.

"Are you back? Lord, I thought you was dead."

"Is it still 1862?" asked Laurie feebly.

"Mad as a hatter. I *should* have stayed outside," muttered the boy.

"I'm not mad," said Laurie, reviving. He sat up in bed, resisting all the boy's efforts to lie him down again. "Listen to me, whoever you are."

"Frank, I told you. Frank Kilderbee."

"Listen. Something very strange is going on. It's weird enough to label me as mad, I know, but I'll tell you the plain truth—what I know of it, which isn't much. Can you believe that tonight I went to bed in Sydney—Sydney, Australia, that is—in the year 1977. I woke up hot . . ."

"Hot?"

"Let's not start that again. I went for a drink. When I came back to bed you were in it and . . . well, here we are. I've tried to believe I'm dreaming, but no dream was ever like this. I don't know what's happening. Do you?"

The boy looked hard at him, a cool, appraising look. Even by moonlight Laurie could tell that he wasn't afraid now.

"No, I don't believe you *are* mad," he said at last.

"Thanks for that, anyway."

"But I don't know what's happened, no more nor you. Sydney, Australia, you say? Didn't they used to send convicts there?"

"Maybe still do," replied Laurie absently, and then continued, more to himself than to Frank, "I've lost a hundred and fifteen years."

"I'll tell you one thing that makes me think maybe you *have* come from another time—those queer clo'es."

"My pajamas?"

"Pajamas?" repeated the boy, grinning for the first time, a small thing that somehow made Laurie feel immeasurably better.

"Pajamas is what I'm wearing. Shortie pajamas. We wear them to bed when it's hot. Don't you?"

"Bless you, I wears what I stands up in, mostly. But what I mean is, not even toffs wear them . . . pajamas. They wears nightshirts."

"So they did . . . do. Oh, Frank, I'm glad it was

25

you who found me. It might have been anyone. I could've been in prison by now!"

"Yiss," said Frank, glowing at Laurie's gratitude. "Course, you might of woke up at home," he hurried on, to escape embarrassment.

"I wonder," said Laurie, and suddenly reaching out behind him, he closed his hand over something smooth and hard and round, like a deep-frozen snowball. "I knew it," he said triumphantly. "This is the link. There had to be one. This is the bed I went to bed in."

"Is it, just?"

"Let me think. The bed. Something about the bed. A sort of warp in time, because of the bed."

"I never heard of such a thing."

"No more did I. I don't suppose it happens very often."

"Are you stuck here now then?"

That question had, of course, been at the back of Laurie's mind since he came to. "I don't know," he answered forlornly, fighting back rising panic again.

A quick, sideways glance showed Frank that comfort was needed. "The bed brought you, p'raps it will take you home again," he suggested.

"You think so?"

"I'm no schollard, but it's all we got to go on, innit?"

"Yes . . . and if that doesn't work, I'm sure I don't know what else to try."

"You'd best stay near that 'ere bed, anyways. It won't be light for a long time yet. You'll be all right."

"Aren't you going to stay with me?"

"I mustn't get caught. They'd set the Peelers on me. I only come 'cause of the cold."

"And me letting you stand there all this time! Here, sit down. Wrap this rug around you. You said yourself it won't be light for ages yet."

Frank looked at him oddly. "You mean it?"

"Why wouldn't I?"

"Why . . . you're a gent, that's why."

"A gent?" Desperate as he was, Laurie couldn't help a brief, nervous laugh. "Frank, sit down. Please."

Rather stiffly, Frank joined him on the bed. Laurie threw a rug around his shoulders, and pulled the quilt up around both their chins. They sat in silence for a time; so many shocks and so much astonishment compelled silence. But gradually Laurie became aware that Frank was observing him closely. He stirred restlessly.

"If you're going to watch till I disappear in a puff of smoke or something, you'll give me a nervous breakdown. Can't we talk? What's your life like? Tell me."

"Nuffin' much to tell, reely."

"There must be. Remember, it's all new to me."

"Well," said Frank, surrendering reluctantly, "what do you want to know?"

"Where do you live?"

"That's easy. Nowhere."

"What do you mean?"

"I been sleeping round the areas and doorsteps in the Square this last week or so. Before that I slep' in a lodging house in the Ratcliff Highway two nights. Before that I slep' under a boat down by the river— but only for a few nights. Before that I . . ."

"Wait a minute. Where's your home? Where's your family?"

"No home. No family. Leastways, I have a father. He's prob'ly still alive. . . . I dunno for sure."

Laurie was aghast. "You don't know?"

"I runned away, you see," said Frank simply, seeing an explanation was required.

"Why?"

"Mother died when I was, oh, little. Little sister died, too. Father was always drunk. He took up with this woman what owned a public house. Even took me to live there—but she didn't want me around, she had me 'prenticed to a chimney sweep. Father didn't care, it mattered more to him to keep in with her. My master was bad. Very bad. After a year I runned away, and worked my way down to London."

"Where from?"

"Leicester."

"Oh," said Laurie, who'd heard of Leicester Square, from the Monopoly board, but supposed this must be somewhere different. "What do you mean, 'worked your way'?"

29

"I picked up a penny where I could, you know, mainly singing outside public houses. Once I worked two weeks on a farm near Aylesbury. Things weren't too sharp at times. Sometimes I'd get a bed and a loaf at the workhouse. Mostly I skippered in barns and under hedges. Sometimes I stole turnips out of fields," he finished, lowering his voice, as though half hoping Laurie wouldn't hear this bit.

"How long did it take to reach London?" asked Laurie, wide-eyed.

"A long time. Three months, maybe. I dursen't show myself too freely, like, in case my master had a trace out for me."

Laurie was stunned. "And what did you do when you got here? How do you live?"

"It was hard. I didn't know what to do. I sang a bit. Tumbled with it, too, till I hurt my ankle. 'Duck-legged Dick' always went over well. You know that?"

"No, I don't think so."

Frank looked surprised. "*You* know. 'Duck-legged Dick had a donkey.'"

"No."

"P'raps it hasn't reached the Colonies yet," said Frank grandly, and Laurie could hardly restrain a smile, in spite of everything.

"'Mother, Is the Battle Over?' was always a go-er, too," continued Frank reflectively, before shrugging his shoulders and moving on to other things. "Oh, then I sold watercress, but it was such a long day, for so little. Up at four to get to Farringdon Market, out

30

all day, and sometimes not the price of my supper at the end of it."

"Lord!"

"Then I thought, them crossing sweepers, *they* don't have to get up afore light. Maybe if I could find an empty crossing, and work up a bit of a connection, like carrying parcels and opening cabs and that, as well as sweeping, I might get a bit forrarder."

"You'll think me stupid, but please, what's a crossing sweeper?"

Frank was scandalized. "Lor', what a place that Sydney must be! Crossing sweepers sweep the roads to make a path clear of dirt and dust and mud for the gentry to cross. Everyone knows that."

"Oh. And did you find a crossing?"

"Right here in the Square. Funny how it happened, reely," Frank continued, warming to the subject. "The old bloke as used to do it was knocked with a carriage. Getting too slow, poor old codger. He's in the workhouse now. I saw it happen meself, while I was holding a horse outside number fifteen. Straight off, I called a boy over as was passing, and arst him to take the horse, and the money, when the gentleman returned, which he was glad to do. Then I runned straight off and bought a broom—see, I *had* three-pence, marvelous how it all worked out, innit?—and I was back on the crossing, all out of breath, in just no time at all. And I been there since September, an' I'll stay there, too."

Frank seemed proud of this part of his story, and

finished in a glow, watching for Laurie's reaction. Laurie felt the bright glance even through the gloom but he didn't know what to say. It was all so strange, so wrong. His instinct was to be outraged by the non-appearance of the child welfare people, but Frank seemed to accept so naturally that he had only himself to rely on, that questions about the inefficiency of the "proper authorities" seemed too silly even to put into words. Obviously there *were* no proper authorities.

"How old are you, Frank?"

Frank's face fell. Was this all the response his enterprise brought?

"I don't rightly know. About half past twelve."

Laurie smiled.

"What did I say? Tell us, what did I say?" demanded Frank hotly.

"Nothing, nothing," replied Laurie quickly. "It's just that . . . we use the language a bit differently in my time, that's all. It's bound to happen. I probably sound fun . . . odd to you at times, too."

"A bit," mumbled Frank, peeping through his lashes to see if Laurie really meant it. His quick resentment puzzled Laurie, till a probable explanation struck him.

"You did say you'd never been to school, didn't you?"

"Yiss."

"Wouldn't you like to?"

There was a pause, then Frank turned quite different eyes on him, eyes that were sick with shame and longing. Laurie understood at once.

"You want it very much, don't you?"

"You don't know how much!" he burst out so passionately that Laurie was taken aback. "You don't know what it is to know nothing. How could you? I can't read. I can't even write my name. I can't read a street sign or newspaper or nothing. I'm only fit for sweeping streets or begging from people who haven't half my wit. I'm not stupid, you know. But I have no chance, none, none at all!"

Laurie was shocked and embarrassed to see two hot tears in Frank's eyes. He put his hand out and softly touched the bundle of quilt where he judged Frank's arm to be.

"Don't cry, Frank. Please don't. You'll learn to read somehow. No one can want something as much as you want that, and not get it." As he spoke. Laurie desperately hoped this was so.

Frank wriggled his arms out into the open, darted his hands quickly across his eyes, and looked as though he regretted his outburst.

"Yiss," he answered shortly, afraid to trust himself further.

In the silence that followed, each became aware of sounds above them. Someone was stirring.

"I tell you, Mr. Questing, I heard a noise downstairs not two minutes since. It's thieves, I know it is."

A deeper voice rumbled something in reply.

"I'm not imagining this time," returned the first voice huffily. "Oh, hurry, do. What if I'm right? What would Master say?"

Frank and Laurie looked at each other in horror. Laurie could feel his scalp prickling, and while one part of his mind was numb with fright, another part was carefully registering that books were right about this too—hair *could* stand on end.

"They're coming," hissed Frank, leaping off the bed.

"What will we do?" whispered Laurie, bouncing after him.

"No time to reach the stairs," returned Frank, casting his eyes around the room. He was tense, but had a coolness that Laurie could only envy. He realized that Frank was much better acquainted with danger than he.

"The wardrobe," was Frank's decision. "Not very good, unless he don't look too hard, but it's our only chance."

He crossed the room swiftly and soundlessly, Laurie two steps behind him, and pulled the wardrobe door wide open. A whiff of mothballs hit them. The wardrobe was thickly hung with clothes, and the floor was piled with boxes, toys, and folded, anonymous garments.

"A bit of a squeege," whispered Frank, beginning to push his way in.

Laurie, dancing about impatiently behind him,

heard steps on the stairs. A grumbling voice said, "If you're wrong again, Flora, watch out, that's all."

"Oh, Mr. Questing, I'm sure. I don't mean to disturb you. Only I did hear something."

Laurie stood transfixed. In a matter of seconds—much less time than it takes to tell—and with the sound of the approaching footsteps in his ears, a riot of thoughts raced through his mind: there was hardly time to bundle into the wardrobe without being heard, and the interior of the wardrobe being as it was, there probably wasn't room for two anyway; it was essential that Frank remain undetected; that only left the bed.

He raced back and tried to get under it, but it was impossible—two wooden chests effectively barred the way. He was lost indeed. The stairs had been left behind, and the footsteps seemed to be advancing along a hall or landing of some sort. They must be nearly upon him. He jumped into the bed and buried himself under the bedclothes. His heart was thudding and the blood was pounding in his ears so that he was momentarily deaf to sounds outside his burrow. He knew it was a stupid thing to do; his other self left him in no doubt of that. "Idiot," it said. "What on earth did you do that for? You're like a little kid who hides under the table and thinks he's invisible. Only these grown-ups aren't going to cooperate and pretend they can't see you."

The deafness faded, and he heard the doorknob

turn. So this was it. He closed his eyes tight, tensed his whole body and waited. And waited. He had read of moments that "seemed to last forever," had even experienced a few, but this was a "forever" of quite another order. "A horse of a different color" flashed ridiculously through his mind as his body grew stiff from being tensed in a tight ball for so long. There was the matter of air, too. Rosie could stay under the blankets for hours without any trouble, but he wasn't Rosie. What was keeping them? They must see the mound under the bedclothes. It was so silent, too. They must be standing there, gloating. How abominable of them! He threw back the blankets indignantly, ready for anything rather than endless waiting. Bright moonlight streamed over him, and a warm breeze swelled the curtains in his own small bedroom.

"Excuse me," said Laurie. "Can you tell me where I can find out when education became compulsory in England?"

It was a young and keen library assistant to whom he applied. She beamed her approval of his end-of-school-year industry, and very quickly found an article on the history of English education in an encyclopedia. Laurie soon found what he wanted. 1870. Too late for Frank. He'd be twenty by then—or half past nineteen. He smiled at the memory.

"What are you smiling at?" asked his acquaintance of the day before. Clare, her name was. Clare Elliot.

"Oh, nothing," said Laurie, watching the approach of the same assistant with a trolley load of books.

"Did you find it?" she asked cheerfully.

"Yes, thank you. I wonder . . . could you tell me where I'd find out when transportation of convicts to Sydney ended?"

She looked at him doubtfully. Such a different subject from the first. Was he being frivolous?

"Earlier than in some other places," she answered guardedly. "About 1840, I think. Any Australian history would tell you—that's downstairs at 994—or the *Australian Encyclopedia* over here. Look up 'Transportation' or 'Convicts' in the index."

"Thank you."

"Surely you're not doing a project, with school breaking up so soon?" she asked, unable to restrain her curiosity.

"No. It's just . . . well, general interest really."

"Very general."

Clare was looking bored. "Aren't you coming down to the fiction? I thought you liked fiction."

"I do, better than anything."

"Come on, then."

"Just a minute. One more thing. Excuse me," he called to the same assistant, who'd moved off with her trolley.

"Yes?" she asked, almost fearfully.

"I'm sorry to trouble you, but could you tell me where I'd find something about a street in London called St. Mary Axe?"

Naturally Laurie thought about his strange adventure. In fact he seldom thought of anything else. How had it happened? Why? In desperation he tried again to persuade himself that it had been just a very real dream, but he couldn't convince himself of that any more than he had been able to during the night. It *had* happened, but no amount of puzzling brought any answers, and there was no one to whom he could turn for help. No one would believe him.

He slept on the divan with Rosie while his room was being redecorated, and he often wondered what would happen when he returned to his own bed. Could it happen again? One moment the possibility excited him, the next moment he tingled with fright at the very idea.

While his feelings veered this way and that, one thing at least remained steady—his concern for Frank, alone in a desperately unfair and uncaring world. It was upsetting to think about, but think he must; and these were the times when he was almost sure he wanted the same queer kink to take him back to London to see how Frank was getting on, even to help him. Not that he counted on it by any means. The magic, or whatever, might have played itself out in that one night; or, if it were still there, might whisk him to some other time and place. Who knew what the bed's history had been? It might have come to Australia via any number of places. And anyway, supposing he did get back to Cavendish Square, what good would it do? Frank wouldn't be beside him in bed; it would be very unlikely that he'd risk that again. So he would be outside somewhere, and even from the window London had seemed grim, alien, and dauntingly full of difficulties.

So he reasoned, and when the room was finally ready, his feelings still vacillated between a desire to see what would happen and a fervent hope that things would remain comfortably normal. When four nights went by uneventfully, he began to think that was that and, contrarily, was half disappointed, telling himself he *would* have liked more adventures after all. On the fifth night, at bedtime, he stood thoughtfully at the foot of the bed, soothing the sand-fly bites on his hands by holding them against each of the three cool balls in turn, as he wondered whether certificates filed with Somerset House in London could provide him with any information about Frank—when he died, for instance. Laurie had discovered that life expectancy in those days was short, especially for the very poor. It would be something to know Frank had reached a good old age. If he had, his life could have extended well into the lifetime of Laurie's own parents. If he was twelve in 1862, he had been born in 1850. Say he lived to be a hundred—it wasn't impossible—he would have died in 1950. Laurie's father had been born in 1930. Even if Frank had died at eighty, their life-spans would have overlapped. He was much taken with this thought, clasping and unclasping his hands around the white ball as he worked on the mathematics of the problem. Unfortunately his flow of thought was interrupted by the entrance of his mother, who had come to say good night, but he resumed, as soon as she'd gone, by flashlight. He felt he couldn't sleep till he'd drafted his letter to Somerset House. "I have reason to suppose Mr. Kilderbee a connection of mine" sounded very grand. It would be best to type the letter and sign it "L. Langridge," as though it came from an adult. He fell asleep thinking he must ask at the library for the address of Somerset House, or wherever it was you had to send.

Some hours later he was jolted awake by a noise, and had some bitter but rather sleep-stupid thoughts about noisy neighbors till his awakening brain began to send out urgent signals about that particular noise. A most unusual noise, when he came to think about it, almost like. . . . He felt the same sensation you get from a rapid descent in an elevator, a peculiar, stomach-left-behind feeling, as he jumped out of bed and sprang to the window. He knew what he would find before he got there. The coldness of the painted floor under his bare feet told him; the look merely confirmed it. He was in London again, it could well be 1862, and the noise that had disturbed him was a carriage and four that had rolled up to a brilliantly lit house on the opposite side of the Square.

His head swam, but only for a moment; then his brain began ticking over, coolly considering the situation. Just two possibilities presented themselves. He could hop into bed—it was his bed, after all—and sleep himself home again, or he could go outside and look for Frank. Hadn't he said he'd been sleeping in the Square recently? If it was still December, 1862—which he couldn't be certain of, though things seemed much the same and Master Pemberton was apparently still away with the croup, whatever that was—then he was possibly not far away. Laurie pressed his nose against the glass and peered down into the Square, but it was too dark to make anything out very clearly. Was it just his consciousness of not belonging that made the world outside seem so menacing? Many times he had looked at a picture that intrigued him—usually of another time and place—and ached with longing to be able to step into it. He was in that position now. The window was the frame, London the picture. Only this time he could step into the picture. "Here's a go," he kept repeating to himself, tingling all over with fright and excitement.

There was no question but that he would go outside, and he ought to go quickly, before too much thinking undermined his small store of courage. He was on his way to the door when he realized he was wearing short cotton pajamas, and had no shoes. He'd been too keyed up to notice the cold till then, but of course he couldn't go out like that. Not only would he catch his death of pneumonia—if he could die before he was born—but he'd probably be arrested as well. First problem. He stood irresolute, and then remembered the wardrobe. Standing behind Frank that other morning he'd seen lots of stuff in there. He tip-toed across to it.

It was crammed with a mixture of male and female clothing, summery things mainly. Groping away in the near-dark he discovered a number of outfits—sailor suits and what-have-you—so peculiar that he could scarcely conceive of anyone's wearing them. He finally settled on a bulky, brown overcoat sort of thing, and put it on right over his pajamas. In doing so, he found his flashlight in his pajama shirt pocket, where he must have slipped it as he felt himself drifting off to sleep. Well, it could be useful at that. In a drawer he found short black stockings and pulled them on, too. In a cupboard he found a collection of boots and shoes, all rather small, but eventually he found some black, shiny ones that would do, "in a pinch," he thought, grinning lopsidedly at his own joke. All in all, he thought he must cut a pretty comical figure—but no more comical than Frank had looked in his assorted, ill-fitting garments.

Having tried the shoes on, he took them off again for the journey to the front door. He felt his way to the bedroom door and opened it silently. Last time he hadn't gone outside the room at all, so he didn't know what to expect. It was very dark, but he could make out a stairway just across the passage. He gripped the banister tightly and began the descent. At the half-landing he let his breath out audibly, and realized he'd been holding it from the head of the stairs. Taking another deep breath, he set off again, now with a mad compulsion to count the stairs. Ten of them—not creaky, fortunately. Things improved in the hall, as faint patches of grayish light in the glass panels of the front door pointed the way for him, and a carpet runner made his advance rapid and silent.

The door itself was likely to be problem number two. There was a heavy bolt to be slipped. How to do it noiselessly? He gave a little tentative tug. Nothing happened. He pulled harder. There was a grinding sound, not too loud, but enough to make him contort his face in the pained way people do when they're trying to be silent. He listened hard for a minute, but there was no stir in the house. The second pull had done the trick and the bolt slid smoothly after that, but he took it very, very gently. Then there was the key to be turned and the knob after it. He felt the cold morning air hit his face as he carefully drew the door back a few inches. There seemed to be no one around. Nevertheless, he must not open the door too wide, just in case. He slipped out through the smallest space possible, and eased the door almost but not quite shut behind him. With the family away and the servants not having to attend the front door much, it just might remain unnoticed, if it didn't blow open. Now it was done. He stood on the top step breathing hard for a time, recovering from one effort and nerving himself for the next. Problem three: to find Frank, somewhere in this dark, unknown city that couldn't feel more alien if it were Mars itself. Squaring his shoulders, he descended the three steps to street level, and launched himself upon London.

He must not panic. He must try to look as though it were the most normal thing in the world to be out walking at dawn, 13,000 miles from home, and one hundred and three years before he was born. The people behind all those windows, what were they like? What time did they get up? What did they eat for breakfast? What did they *do*? He couldn't imagine.

Sometimes he shone his flashlight down into the basement courts called "areas," but only briefly, and after listening carefully for any sounds of activity below the stairs. It would be hard to explain that flashlight if he were caught.

When he'd covered two sides of the Square he heard footsteps ringing out ahead of him on the frosty pavement, and his heart skipped a beat. His instinct was to turn and run, but he nerved himself onward, feigning a casual, sauntering pace. He glanced at the man out of the corner of his eye as they passed. He hadn't meant to, but was irresistibly drawn to look at this, his second specimen of nineteenth-century life. Also, he wanted to see what reaction, if any, his own eccentric appearance aroused.

"Mornin'," said the man, with, as far as Laurie could see, no change of expression at all.

"Mornin'," replied Laurie, careful to reproduce the

same tone and accent. The man went on, dragging a ladder beside him. Why? Laurie felt there were going to be lots of "whys" in this episode of his life.

After he'd made a complete round, looking at all the doorsteps and in the areas, he crossed to the center of the Square to think. There, sitting on a bench, he was soon listening to the morning song of the birds in the trees around him, wondering at the same time whether the satisfaction of knowing would be worth the effort involved in counting the enormous number of chimney pots within view. He was turning this question over in his mind when he was interrupted.

"Laurie?"

He turned around quickly. Frank.

"It is Laurie, ain't it?" asked Frank anxiously, as Laurie, stricken dumb, just stared.

"Yes, it's me," said Laurie, rousing himself. "I've been looking for you, Frank, all around the Square."

"I've just come," Frank answered simply, holding up his broom as evidence that he'd only just arrived on the job.

They were both rather tongue-tied at this sudden meeting. Yet there was so much each wanted to know about the other.

"This is the first time I've been back since that other morning," said Laurie, breaking the silence.

"Is it? I wondered whether I'd see you again. I didn't think I would. I wanted to," said Frank jerkily.

Laurie was struck by a thought. "Can it be the marble knobs on the bed, I wonder? I was rubbing them, because of my bites, and . . . here I am."

"Maybe they do set it off then."

"That other time, too. I was cleaning the bed— probably touched the knobs quite a bit. Hang on, though, what happened that other morning?"

"They came in and . . . you just wasn't there. The bed was straight and all. They didn't do no more than just stand in the doorway. Didn't that maid get it, though! I got out the *front door* when that brute of a footman, or whatever he is, thumped up the stairs again, with the maid all in tears behind him."

"So you knew then that I'd spoken the truth?"

"I believe I knew it before then."

"I'm glad." Laurie smiled with real pleasure. It was beginning to come home to him that the event so long thought of was actually taking place. This was really Frank standing here in front of him.

"Well, Frank, how goes it with you?"

"Pretty good, sir . . . I mean Laurie." He grinned as he corrected himself. "I been making up to nine-pence a day lately—one and threepence one day. All the families in the Square are home, see, with Christmas coming. I got a room," he finished grandly.

"Really?"

"In Catherine Wheel Alley. Well, I shares it, but only with one other, and Jubal don't come in till late."

"Who's Jubal?"

47

"Funny old codger. Works at The Bull, Aldgate."

"Is your room far from here?"

"Goodish way. Near Petticoat Lane."

"Oh, I've heard of that."

"Really?"

"Yes. There's a market there in my time."

"Mine too. It's there now." He hesitated, and then continued shyly, "Would you like to see my place?"

"Very much. But wouldn't I be keeping you from your work?"

"It's early—not many people around yet. Aksherly, I wasn't coming at all this morning, for a reason, but then I thought, well, if I go early I jus' might be lucky an' pick up an extra penny or two before . . ." He stopped.

Laurie pretended not to notice that something was being kept from him, and gazed with careful indifference at the lightening sky.

"No, I *will* say it," Frank announced firmly. "I don't know why I didn't straight off. I'm going to school this morning. First time."

"No! That's terrific! Didn't I say you'd get to read and write somehow?"

"Yiss," said Frank, beaming. "I been saving. It's a Ragged School, in Bishopsgate."

He spoke as though "Ragged School" ought to mean something to Laurie. It didn't, but he thought privately that if raggedness was a requirement, Frank filled the bill to a T, despite what he almost seemed to regard as his present affluence.

48

"When you going home?" asked Frank, not shy now.

"I don't know. I'll have to get back inside the house. But later. Now I'm out, I want to see London. I was reluctant inside, but it's like getting into a cold sea, you know. Once you're in, it's great."

This remark was lost on Frank, who'd never seen the sea, let alone been in it. Not that it mattered, since he wasn't listening anyway, being engaged in a scheme of his own.

"You hungry?" he asked suddenly.

"Funny you should mention that. I was just going to, because I *am*."

"Well, what I say is this. We can go and get some breakfast—I know a place—then we can go to my place. It's a fair way. You'll see London. Then at ten o'clock, when I go to school, you can . . ."

"I'll go, too."

"But you *can* read and write."

"I want to see what it's like."

"It's a penny," cautioned Frank.

That stopped Laurie. He didn't have a penny, and he couldn't ask Frank, whose pennies were obviously very precious.

"Oh. Well, I suppose I'd best go home then."

He was disappointed, and Frank sensed it.

"I'll pay for you," he offered quickly.

"Thank you," said Laurie touched. "I'll make it up to you somehow, I promise. And now, breakfast. Oh, blow! I can't pay for that either."

49

"My treat."

"Thanks again. I tell you what, Frank. My flashlight was in my pocket when I went to sleep, so . . ."

"Flashlight?" interrupted Frank, startled.

A vision of what "flashlight" must mean to Frank popped into Laurie's head and he laughed.

"It's not what you think. I'll explain as we go. But what I was getting at is, apparently I can bring things back with me, if they're in my pockets—or if I'm holding them, presumably. Next time—if there is one—I'll bring back something we can sell, and then I'll repay you."

"No need. I'm doing well. I told you."

"I know, but I *want* to. Now, where's this place for breakfast?"

"Billingsgate. Rodway's."

"Billingsgate! I've heard of that, too. It's a fish market."

"So it is. My eye, I don't see what you've got to learn about London—you know it all already!"

They both laughed.

"This is grand!" exclaimed Frank. "I declare a holiday! Oh, *aren't* I glad I come this morning!"

It was a chastened Laurie who sat down with
Frank at Rodway's half an hour later. He had
considered himself ready for anything, but he'd been
shocked by the poverty all around him. Before they'd
set out he had thought Frank's mode of dress quite
exceptionally tatty, but since then he had seen so many
coatless, shirtless, even shoeless people; so many whose
clothes hung in strips; so many in garments so almost
comically overlarge or small that they had obviously
begun life on different backs, that he now realized
that, for a particular class of Londoner, Frank was the
norm rather than the exception. Not a small class, at
that.

"Tell me this, Frank," he began, rather truculently,
because he was badly shaken. "Why does every man,
woman, and child in this city wear something on their
head?"

"Why?" repeated Frank, all surprise. "They just do. It's on'y natural."

"Why?"

"Well," said Frank, who'd obviously never given it a moment's thought in his life, "people have a betterly appearance in a hat, don't they?"

"I only thought," continued Laurie, "that when you can barely afford to cover yourself, there seems more point in spending money on a scarf or shoes, than a hat. I mean, bare feet, in this climate!"

Frank looked unconvinced, but the subject lapsed, as Laurie's attention moved to other things; and certainly Rodway's was an interesting place. It was still early, but the market had been bustling and busy long since. There was a powerful odor of fish and the river outside, and it penetrated inside as well, especially about the persons of the market workers who had come to have their breakfast. Coffee and two slices of bread and butter cost a penny, and the coffee-house was conducted on what Frank seemed to consider, with some pride, as superior lines. There were long lines of plain wooden chairs and tables, and a wooden floor. The atmosphere was quiet and purposeful—people came to eat, that was all, and soon returned to the highly organized confusion outside. Mr. Rodway himself, very grand, surveyed the room from the end, and made sure that standards were maintained. Laurie enjoyed his breakfast, but would have liked more.

Afterward, on their way to Frank's room, they passed through the Petticoat Lane market. It was as active as Billingsgate, and even more crowded. Rows of old clothes were suspended on lines above head level, and there were hundreds of stalls, from superior-looking carts down through tables to barrows to small heaps of knives, nails, scissors, and candles on the ground. Wandering sellers called their wares. Most strident of all, Laurie could hear "Three pairs for a halfpenny, bootlaces," "Penny a lot, fine russets," "All new nuts, penny a half-pint." He wondered what half a pint of nuts could possibly mean, but there wasn't time to ask Frank because next moment he had to consider what "chonkeys" and "jumbles" might be. They looked and smelled good. "Jam tarts" he had no trouble recognizing.

Catherine Wheel Alley was not much further. It was one of a maze of streets, lanes, rows, passages, alleys, yards, courts, and places in the Petticoat Lane area. Laurie wondered how anyone found their way home, or, once home, out again. The little room Frank shared with the absent Jubal was at the top of a decrepit building, full of dark, greasy-walled passages. The room was not small, but having said that, there was nothing else that could be said for it. The one window, broken and stuffed with bits of board and paper, looked across a tiny court to a similar drunken, leaning tenement. There was a bed, one broken chair, a table—no other furnishings. There was a fireplace, but no fire, nor any sign of one. Above the mantelpiece were two small, curling pictures, to which Frank immediately drew Laurie's attention. One, a ship, had been torn from a magazine; the other, a dog of no known breed, had been drawn by Frank himself. These two pictures were his contribution to the interior decoration of the room, and as such he was proud of them. Laurie knew he was expected to admire them and did so, thinking uncomfortably of his room at home.

"Do you have a fire here? Where do you cook?"

"There's a kitchen down below, with a good fire. We can sit there at night. You can cook a bit of fish, or toast some bread, or what you like. And make tea. We have some good times there, you'd better believe." Frank didn't sound as though *he* believed it.

Laurie was trying hard, but it was difficult to keep all trace of shock out of his eyes and voice. Frank felt it, and was hurt; he supposed Laurie must be very rich indeed.

"Course, if I'd had more paper, I could of done a better dog," he said. "That was my first go."

"It's a good dog. I like the dog," said Laurie miserably. Then, stirring himself to be a better guest, added, "I have a cat, you know. Rosie."

"Have you?" said Frank, with more than polite interest. "What's she like? Is she pretty?"

"She's gray and white. She's pretty, when she's not being grumpy. She's grumpy now—you see, we've just

54

moved, and she can't work out what's happened. She's getting better though. Last night she ate a big dinner." The fact that it was probably a good deal bigger than Frank's occurred to Laurie as he said it.

"It must be good to have a cat or a dog. Next to learning to read and write, that's what I'd like most."

"Is it really?" asked Laurie in surprise. "Oh, yes," was the heartfelt reply.

Since Frank was anxious to be on time for school they didn't remain long in his room, for which Laurie was grateful. He was cold, and the room—the whole court or yard or whatever it was—depressed him greatly. Ten minutes of brisk walking brought them to the hall in Bishopsgate where the school was held. A large number of scholars—ragged children all, some minding even younger brothers and sisters—was already assembled, and while they waited Laurie looked about him. It was another bare-floored, grim interior, with a high, beamed ceiling, and huge texts painted along the side walls. One side read, "Go to the ant, thou sluggard. Proverbs 6:6"; the other, "Wisdom is better than rubies. Proverbs 8:11."

At one minute to ten a straight-backed, cold-eyed man advanced down the center of the hall, followed by three earnest-looking women and a plump, curly-haired man carrying some books. Laurie was aware of Frank stirring excitedly beside him, and was glad to be there with him.

The first man was apparently a clergyman, and a

very important person in the affairs of the school. He gave a little speech about the tremendous privilege it was for the children to be there, and how they should all be grateful. He made them repeat two little verses till they had them by heart.

Honest work is always holy
howsoever hard and lowly
and
Envy not the rich and great,
wealthier in your low estate,
nobler through your workful days,
happier in your simple ways.

Laurie repeated the verses with the other children, half embarrassed and half angry. He didn't like the man. He didn't like the way he made it abundantly clear that a great gulf was fixed between him and his poor, uncritical listeners. A half-glance at Frank showed that his eyes were shining, *he* wasn't offended. Worse was to come. Now they were getting a sermon.

". . . God, in His infinite wisdom, has appointed a place for every man, woman, and child on this earth, and it is their bounden duty to remain contentedly in their niches. A gentleman might seem to have a pleasant, easy life, compared to a poor man's, but he has his duties and responsibilities, which would be far beyond your capabilities. He has to pay taxes, sit on the Bench of Magistrates, oversee his property, and keep up his position by entertaining. Could a poor man do these things? No, of course not; and I do not suppose that a gentleman could dig ditches or scrub floors as well as the lower orders."

The children beamed, gratified that the gentleman considered them good for something. Laurie burned.

". . . So may you and your families be thankful and rejoice in your physical strength and the bounty of your betters, who find you work and pay you wages with their own money and . . ."

"Rubbish!" shouted Laurie.

As though he were someone else, he was aware that he had stood up. He felt Frank freeze beside him. It seemed as though hundreds of round, astonished eyes were fixed on him.

"What is the meaning of this?" came icily from the proud clergyman.

"Just this. Who do you think you are, telling all these people to be content with hunger and cold and ignorance and poverty and hats [Laurie was getting a bit confused here] and calling it God's will? If you had any regard for God's will you couldn't bear for such conditions to exist around you, let alone be complacent about them."

"So I'm complacent, am I?"

"That's what I'd call it. I don't know what *you* call it."

There were horrified gasps all around. The children clasped each other and looked frightened. Frank was scrabbling at his arm, urging him down.

The clergyman was very, very angry, but not entirely sure how to proceed. He was not used to being contradicted. This was not a situation he'd ever imagined in his wildest dreams. While he was momentarily silenced Laurie seized the initiative again.

"According to you, my friend here [indicating Frank, who sat back weakly, moaning something like 'Oh, my Gawd'] must be a crossing sweeper all his life and like it, although he probably has the intelligence to be a nuclear physicist. Hold on, a . . . a poet laureate," he corrected himself, remembering where he was and substituting something that sounded more Victorian. "Whereas, you might have a son at home pure wood from ear to ear. Is *he* going to be a crossing sweeper? Is Frank going to get *his* place at university? Not on your life! I ask you, is that God's will? Is that *fair*?"

Laurie ran out of steam, but continued to glare fiercely around.

"Sandys, get rid of that loutish boy," hissed the clergyman, white with anger.

"Yes sir, Mr. Cumberland," replied the plump little man, his voice almost a squeak from nervousness.

"Don't worry, I wouldn't stay for the world," retorted Laurie, to Mr. Sandys' infinite relief.

"*And* his friend the poet laureate. Such a brilliant young man can have no need of our poor school," continued Mr. Cumberland, as though Laurie had not spoken. It was only then that Laurie realized what he'd done. With burning cheeks, Frank rose and followed him past all the silent, watching children and out to Bishopsgate.

"I'm sorry, Frank," whispered Laurie.

Frank sighed. "You meant it for the best," he mumbled, in an embarrassed sort of way.

"Yes, but it was your chance. You wanted it so much."

"Well, I didn't get it. Serves me right. Learning isn't meant for the likes of me. It was a dream, that's all."

Laurie's ire rose again. Heavens, what's come over me, he thought, as he found himself shaking Frank's shoulders roughly.

"Stop thinking like that. Of course you've a right to education. Why, in another eight years everyone will, by law."

"Is that a fac'?" asked Frank in surprise.

"Yes. So you see, the world is changing. Soon . . ." He stopped, and a new expression came into his eyes.

"Yes?" Frank could see something was up.

Laurie didn't answer for a moment. Then he snapped his fingers decidedly. "We're a right pair, Frank. Here we are carrying on as though the world had ended, when there's a very simple solution."

"I wish I knew it."

"*I'll* teach you, that's what. Probably better than they could, too," with a nod to the building behind them.

Frank just stared, but Laurie could see new hope dawning.

"If you *could*," he whispered feelingly.

"Of course I could. And free, too."

"But what if you don't come back no more?"

"I feel sure I will. Maybe this is the point of the whole thing. Maybe I was meant to teach you. Think of it!"

A big grin was Frank's answer this time.

"Well, you've taken the morning off, so we might as well begin. Is there somewhere near here we could go? Not far—my feet hurt."

"See that church there—St. Ethelburga's, I think it's called—there's a little churchyard behind it. It's quiet. We could go there."

They did, and there, in the cold winter morning, Frank had his first lesson. They had neither pencil nor paper, so Laurie drew with a stick on the ground.

"See that, Frank, that's an A."

It wasn't an easy decision for Laurie, to tell Clare what had happened or to keep silent. Their friendship—only it could hardly be called that yet—proceeded jerkily. Sometimes he was almost unbearably irritated by her prissiness, her certainty, her tendency to be right; then she would say something that proved she'd seen to the heart of a much-loved book, or do something that showed a careful respect for Rosie's nerves, and he would feel a warm rush of liking for her. He blew hot and cold, and there it was.

Finally he did tell her. It was Christmas Eve, and they were sitting in the apricot tree. An embarrassing business it was, too, with Laurie shredding leaves intently the whole time, to avoid looking at Clare. His voice was flat, almost bored, with only the occasional hoarseness of strain to show how very far from bored he was in fact feeling. Inside himself he was thinking

he could always pass it off as a joke if the story mis-
fired, as it almost certainly would. Stupid girl. Mad-
ness to have begun.

Clare was quiet when he'd finished, and continued
chewing at a leaf calmly, as though he'd been as dreary
as the adults when they went on about boring things
such as whether you had more a look of your Uncle
Jack or Auntie Beth. Then she spoke.

"If what you're wearing goes back with you, you
should wear warm things that Frank can keep. They
might just fade away when you come back, but it's
worth a try. They should be clothes suitable to the
times. I'll make some."

At that moment, Laurie liked her a lot.

He was sent to bed soon after tea. It was tremendously unjust, Christmas Eve and all, but it was only
by resting first that he'd be allowed to go to Midnight
Mass at Christ Church St. Laurence, and he'd set his
heart on that. He clumped up the stairs heavily, to
show his aggrieved feelings, and took Rosie with him
for comfort.

"It's ridiculous. I won't sleep," he assured her, cir-
cling his fingertips gently behind her ears as she lay
along his chest and stomach. She just stared, dribbling
ecstatically and jutting her head forward so that he'd
scratch her under her chin. He breathed deeply, be-

cause Rosie enjoyed riding up and down his chest. She liked a rocky ride—often she'd start purring when he tossed around in bed—and Laurie had a theory that she'd been a ship's cat in a previous life. Perhaps it was the deep, steady breathing, anyway something slipped him off to sleep, despite his protestations, and he didn't wake till he felt Rosie nudging her way under the blankets. That meant she was cold, and *that* meant they were in London. Both of them!

It seemed to be about the same time as he'd left behind. Looking out the window he saw more activity than on his previous visits. There were people in the Square, lights in the houses; two carriages passed as he watched. Was it Christmas Eve here, too? His eyes fastened on Frank, standing at the crossing with his broom, blowing on his hands as he waited for customers. That was a stroke of luck, because he could never ever have found his way to Catherine Wheel Alley alone. He couldn't take Rosie outside with him, of course, so he made what he hoped was an irresistibly comfortable nest for her on the bed, and lifted her in to it. Then he slipped on the same outfit he'd worn before, thinking that he must wear shoes to bed in the future, since Master Pemberton's tight pumps were a bit much. But what if he died in the night and in the morning they found him in bed with his shoes on?

He edged into the hall and listened for sounds of activity in the house. There were none. At least, there

64

was one—an anxious yowl from Rosie, scrabbling fran-
tically at the door behind him. He quickly pushed it
open, and entreated her to be quiet. She allowed him
to pick her up and resettle her on the bed.

"There," he whispered. "Good girl. You stay here.
Look, it's lovely and warm." She gazed up at him
fondly, and was back at the door half a step ahead of
him.

"Oh, Lord," Laurie groaned. There seemed to be
nothing to do but take her, because if she set up a
racket and they discovered her, they'd bundle her out
into the street for sure, and, panicking, she'd very
likely take off where he'd never find her again.

Every instinct warning him that no good could
come of it—only the alternative seemed rather worse
—he wrapped her tightly in one of Master Pemberton's nightshirts, so that her freedom of movement
was restricted, and folded one side of his coat around
her. She was quite amiable about this, though Laurie
would have expected a great deal of drama and carry-
ing-on. Maddening animals, cats—totally unpredict-
able.

He hurried down the stairs, giving thanks for Master Pemberton's croup, which at least made for a slack,
relaxed household and an unlocked front door. He
could hear voices and thumps from down below—
perhaps the servants were celebrating Christmas—but
there was no difficulty at all in reaching the Square.

Frank was delighted to see him, ecstatic when Rosie

popped her head out. He was pretty excited anyway, since not one but two people had given him sixpence as a Christmas treat, and the Duke of Portland, for whom he regularly ran errands, had given him half a crown! All this, together with the odd threepences and coppers that came his way, had rather gone to his head.

"I've took fourteen and a penny this week—honest! Hap as not I'd get more if I stayed on—Mr. Tremenheere ain't home yet, for one, and he's a reg'lar—but what I say is, let's go to the circus. It's Christmas! I been standing here thinking how I'd like to—I never been—and wishing there was someone I could go with —a friend, like."

"I haven't got any money, Frank. And, anyway, no one would take *my* money."

"*I* have," declared Frank stoutly.

It was settled. Frank stowed his broom down the Duke's area steps, and off they went, with Laurie vowing to himself that this was the last expense Frank would go to on his behalf. He must think of something he could bring back and sell, and make sure he had it every time he went to bed.

It seemed a goodish way to the circus, but it was an exciting time to be out. It was not unpleasantly cold once they got going, and the streets were thronged with good-humored crowds. Laurie almost found himself looking about for Ebenezer Scrooge or Bob Cratchit. They went down Regent Street and up through the Horse Guards to Whitehall and down to the river and the spanking new Houses of Parliament, which Laurie recognized immediately. They crossed the river by Westminster Bridge, the water below them black, thick, and wicked-looking.

"You've got a pollution problem there," said Laurie severely, but Frank didn't understand.

It seemed that Ashley's was their destination—Ashley's Amphitheatre—where a "Classical selection of hippodramatic compositions" was to be presented; either that or *Richard III*. Laurie was a bit hard put to figure out which. When questioned, Frank didn't know either—it was enough for him that he was going to the circus—but he did helpfully point out "A" for "Ashley's" and "A" for "Amphitheatre," plus several other letters that he recognized.

Laurie was surprised and impressed by the interior. It was no circus tent, but a kind of theater, with tiers of seats and boxes around three sides of the ring, a huge central chandelier, and lots of mirrors and gilding and warm red plush. Clean white sawdust covered the ring, and there was a vague smell of horses throughout. The orchestra, between the stage and the circus ring, was already tuning up when they entered, and the long, brilliant row of lights was coming up. Frank and Laurie had paid the cheapest admittance fee, and stood at the back, among a high-spirited, unruly crush of people who were none too fresh. Everyone seemed very fond of oranges, and it appeared to be quite the thing to hurl the peel at friends and strangers alike. Rosie didn't much like the heat and commotion. She wriggled, and mouthed a few soundless meows to Laurie as if to say, "What are we doing here?" He held her close and ducked his head inside his coat, begging her to be a good girl.

The performance was something between a circus as Laurie knew it and a stage show. As well as the usual acrobats and clowns and things, there were comic songs, a ballet, and horses—especially horses, which were worked into the acts in all sorts of likely and unlikely ways. A pretty girl in dark blue spangles, and daringly showing about four inches of leg, sang "The Gypsy Girl," and an ugly man with a nutcracker face sang "Black Your Boots" and "The Rat-Catcher's Daughter." The proceedings were presided over by a riding master, majestic in red coat and high, shiny hat. His manner was that of a stern headmaster at times, and the people near Laurie certainly needed headmastering, though they paid but very little heed. They jostled and were restless, jeered the acts they didn't like and the jokes they'd heard before, and became boisterously excited when their heroes or heroines came on. A few of the leading young bloods appeared to derive quite as much pleasure from showing off in front of their girls and mates as they did from any part of the performance. More than likely this was the main, even the sole purpose for which they'd come.

The finale was an equestrian version of *Richard III*, featuring, so the riding master assured them, "many surprising and peculiar feats of horsemanship." Mr. William Shakespeare would have been very surprised indeed. The story was taken up just before the battle of Bosworth Field. Richard and his adversary, the Earl of Richmond, were encamped and sleeping before the battle, their tents conveniently side by side. Up rose the ghosts of all the people Richard was supposed to have disposed of on his way to the throne— Henry VI and his son; his brother, the Duke of Clarence; Rivers, Grey, and Vaughan—whoever they might be; Lord Hastings; the young princes in the Tower; Richard's own wife; and lastly the Duke of Buckingham. Oddly enough, all the ghosts were on horseback, and all the horses were grays, which must have struck the management as a seemly sort of color for a ghost's horse.

All the specters said horrible things to Richard and encouraged Richmond. The poor ghost of Clarence was rather fat, and when he declaimed, "Let me sit heavy on thy soul tomorrow!" there were cheerful shouts of "Nothing surer, Clarrie!" and "Why don't you pick on someone your own size!" However everyone was quiet when the golden-haired ghosts of the two little princes came on, standing on one gray, and when they said, "Dream on thy cousins smother'd in the Tower . . . thy nephews' souls bid thee despair and die!" some of the hecklers' girls dabbed at their eyes. Laurie could see that Frank was affected, but he himself had other things on his mind—Rosie was becoming very restive, struggling to free her paws from her nightshirt.

Then came morning and the battle. King Richard, in a not very authentic-looking blue-spangled cloak (it looked suspiciously like the one the gypsy girl had worn) came on with Sir William Ratcliff. Sir William, with a wink to the audience, said, "What can I come for to go for to fetch for to bring for to carry for to do for you?" Though Laurie was not familiar with the play, he shook his head dubiously at these words. Somehow it didn't seem like Shakespeare. Richard told Ratcliff to saddle white Surrey, and in a moment on came Surrey, gaily caparisoned and bowing to the audience. Then the battle was on, horses everywhere, clashing of swords, yells. Alarums and excursions, in fact, and great excitement in the audience. Rosie didn't like it one bit. Intent on the action, Laurie didn't notice that she'd worked her front paws loose. Then Surrey was slain, and lay down tidily on the sawdust. King Richard was distraught.

"A horse! A horse! My kingdom for a horse!" he groaned, tearing his hair, and "Done! Your kingdom for my nag Bess!" roared the boldest of the young blades, to the great glee of his friends.

"Withdraw, My Lord," implored one of the king's supporters, "I'll help you to a horse." But the king stood firm and said, "I think there be six Richmonds

70

in the field; five have I slain today instead of him." Then he repeated ringingly, "A horse! A horse! My kingdom for a horse!"

What he got was a cat. Rosie had had enough. Finding herself able to move freely at last, she almost exploded from Laurie's coat, bounded over a few heads and shoulders into the aisle, and then, naturally enough, tore along this clear space. Unfortunately she chose the direction of the ring, and was soon entangled in the opposing armies of King Richard III and the Earl of Richmond, frightening the horses and confusing the action of the battle of Bosworth Field.

"There's your horse. Saddle up, Your Majesty!" hooted a cockney Irishman, nudging Laurie sharply in the ribs. The whole house collapsed with laughter, not just the unruly band around Laurie and Frank.

King Richard froze, his sword dangling limply from his hand, his eyes blank.

In an agony of embarrassment and fright for Rosie's safety, Laurie broke from the crowd, and ran for the ring. He was vaguely aware that Frank was pounding along behind him.

Rosie, terrified by the lights and the noise, backed into dead Surrey, who promptly decided he was alive after all, scrambled to his feet, and bowed, to the roars of the crowd.

"Go it, moggie," yelled someone from the gallery. "Pussy for king. Crown the pussy!" and the call, "Pussy for King," was taken up all over the auditorium.

71

Laurie cornered Rosie, pounced, and clutched her tightly. Everyone cheered. Laurie had by now lost his head as completely as Rosie herself. "She's a girl. She can't be king!" he shouted madly, as though it were necessary to make that clear, and wondered at the new wave of laughter.

"Come on!" hissed Frank, and tugged at his sleeve. Laurie had enough sense left to fly after him up the aisle, just as some official-looking men were advancing threateningly toward them. Somehow they reached the street, and didn't stop running till, clattering down some steps near the bridge, they came to a standstill beside the black, oily depths of the river.

It seems that everywhere you go with me we get pitched out," said Laurie mournfully.

"Never mind, it was almost over," said Frank. "I just only wonder how it ended."

"If it's any comfort, my mother says Shakespeare was all wrong about Richard III. She says he didn't murder those little princes at all."

"Did he kill the . . . the Earl of Richmond?"

"No. The Earl killed *him*, and became king himself. Henry VII, I think, a very mean king."

"Was he Queen Victoria's father then?"

"Father? Frank, Frank, this all happened *hundreds* of years ago!" laughed Laurie.

"Oh," said Frank, turning brick red and glancing away.

Laurie was ashamed. Think, you fool, he scolded himself, say something, make it right. He looked at Rosie, snuggled like a baby in Frank's arms.

"Rosie likes you," he said hurriedly and almost shyly. "She doesn't take to strangers generally."

Frank looked down at his soft, warm burden and smiled, his discomfiture forgotten. Laurie was suddenly struck by the thought that, much as he must long for them, there could be no pets in Frank's life.

They were in a coffeehouse, where they'd gone to get in out of the cold for a few minutes, on their way back to Cavendish Square. It was a grim, low-ceilinged place, with bare boards, gravy-colored walls, a meager fire struggling in an ash-spattered fireplace. The proprietor eyed them suspiciously till Frank produced his penny. Then he became only half surly. Not much Christmas spirit there! They carried their coffee to the furthest booth; away from the apology for a fire, certainly, but safer for Rosie.

Some rooms are capable of reducing the liveliest spirits to gloom and depression within five minutes. This was one, and the dozen or so customers looked pretty far gone. Maybe memories of other Christmases, loneliness, who knows what, contributed to the effect, but Laurie was inclined to think that, in that place, they'd look as glum any night of the year.

He and Frank were in rather better condition than most, though even they had fallen silent. Frank was enjoying Rosie, and Laurie, far from brooding on what might have been, was resolving to be sure of always taking a pencil and paper to bed in the future, since they were losing a valuable opportunity for a lesson. His bed was going to be rather cluttered, one way and another.

As he sat, he was aware that people had slipped into the booth behind him. They had things to say, unlike most of the customers, and gradually Laurie found himself tuning in to their conversation. It was impossible to catch every word over the back of the high booth, but he heard enough.

"I can't understand the delay, that's what I can't understand." This from the louder of the voices, which sounded both surly and aggrieved, as well as a little blurred around the edges, as though from drink.

"I told you, Jem, it isn't easy. There's plans to be made. Arrangements. We need time, boy," answered the other voice, softer and cooler, but thoroughly unpleasant for all that. "Sinister" was the word that popped into Laurie's head, and he felt a shiver run up his spine.

"Time, time, you've had it. It's flown," growled the first voice. "They're coming back, I tell you."

"Yes, yes, Jem," soothed the first voice. "I'm glad you brought me the news. That was well considered of you, very. Such a bitter night too! I'll inform my principal as soon as may be. He'll be grateful to you, you may be sure. Very grateful. How much time have we got?" The voice, though remaining soft, became sharper and harder with the question.

"Dunno. 'e'll let Mrs. B. know when things is settled. 'Master Francis is so much improved,' 'e says, 'that we anticipate a return to London within three weeks at the utmost.' Can't recommend Devon too highly. Says we'll all be charmed to 'ear that Master Francis has become a reg'lar little Hercules down there. Huh! Weedy little prig. And the father not much better."

Laurie's mind was jolted to complete and avid attention by these words. He'd had an idea he'd heard that voice before, but had rejected it as impossible. Now there seemed a strong possibility that this was the servant he'd heard on the stairs that first time in Cavendish Square. By Frank's expression he could tell that the thought had occurred to him also.

"You got any idea how 'e'll pull the job?" resumed the first voice, in a wheedling tone.

"Not me, Jem, no. My principal is a secretive man. Oh yes, very secretive," was the reply. It didn't sound very convincing to Laurie; nor to the questioner, apparently.

"See, I want to be sure nothing can be traced to me. That's natural."

"Oh yes."

"I just wondered, that's all. You can't blame me for that." The servant, if it were he, had the readiness of the drunk to become offended.

"Of course not. I'm not blaming you, Jem," was the smooth reply. "But let me put a case to you, now. Would there be a servant in the house, a young woman, say, who hasn't had her place long—a bit of an unknown quantity, you might say?"

"There's Emmy. Emmy Plover. She come to us not

77

long afore they went away. Why? You know her?"

"I've never heard of her. I just put the case to you. That's very good, that is. Very satisfactory."

"What is?" asked Jem, bemused.

"Is she a good worker, Jem? Nice girl?"

"She's all right. A bit slow, but willing. She's learning."

"See she don't learn too fast, Jem, boy."

"What do you mean?"

"Don't make things too easy for her. Is she by any chance a nervous girl? A bit quiet? Shy?"

"All that. It's her first place, see."

"Better and better. Mind what I say, Jem. Lean on her a bit. Hint to your old biddy of a housekeeper that things is not quite satisfactory with Emmy."

"Why?"

"Oh Jem, Jem, what am I to do with you? Can't you see? Suspicion must fall on her. *She* must be the weak link, and you as innocent as a veritable babe. When's her afternoon off?" The question came sharply, as before.

"Thursday."

"I'll see a young man of my acquaintance gets to meet her. A devilish charming, handsome young rake. Make sure everyone sees them together; make sure everyone knows. Maybe she'll oblige by spreading the word herself if my young dazzler has his usual success. Afterward we'll let it be known, discreetly—discreetly, Jem—that he's a known criminal who's pulled this sort of dodge before. It will be obvious, won't it? Thief woos servant, for love of thief servant provides access to house, house is robbed. Happens all the time, Jem, all the time. You'll be the distraught, faithful servant. Can you manage a little distraughtness, Jem?" he finished, with a short, unpleasant laugh, something between a cough and a hiss, that froze Laurie's blood. He was certain the conspirators didn't know there was anyone in the next booth, and they must not know. There was that in the voice of the soft-spoken man which signified ruthlessness, cruelty, danger.

Now, having received the news of the return of the owners to the house which was to be robbed, he appeared to have no desire to continue in the company of his informant. Quietly, firmly, he took his leave, pursued clumsily by the treacherous servant, still seeking assurances and confidences that his companion was by no means minded to give him.

As their footsteps receded, Laurie warily raised his head and peeped over the back of the booth. The men had their backs to him, but he could see that one was heavily built and the other—the owner of the soft voice, he was certain—small and wiry, with soft, smooth movements to match his voice.

"Well!" he said, turning back to Frank with a sigh of relief.

"The Pembertons, do you think?" asked Frank, who, nursing Rosie, had not shared Laurie's brief glimpse of the departing men.

"Sounds like it. Do you know what their butler, or whatever he is, looks like?"

"I s'pose I must have seen him, but not to take notice."

"Should we follow him? We're going to Cavendish Square anyway. If he heads in that direction, we can see where he goes."

"Good idea."

Rosie was returned to Laurie, to be tucked inside Master Pemberton's coat, which was a great deal warmer than Frank's threadbare jacket. Then they hurried out into the street and looked about them. The small man had melted into the night, which somehow didn't surprise them, but the big one could be seen weaving unsteadily toward the Haymarket. Laurie and Frank followed. Far from sober and totally unsuspicious, he was an easy mark. Indeed, the boys almost wished him sober as a judge as, chafing with impatience, they matched their pace to his shambling, uncertain steps. They couldn't help feeling conspicuous—it was hardly the weather for a stroll.

In the Haymarket he disappeared into a gin palace. There was nothing to do but wait, stamping up and down and blowing on their hands, jostled by crowds on their way to and from theaters, supper rooms, and music halls. Gaslight threw a sick yellow tinge on the faces of garishly-painted women and their bold-eyed escorts, and emphasized the hollow eyes and cheeks of the men, women, and children who, even at this hour

THE ROYAL N⁰ HAYMARKET 4 POTATO CAN

and on Christmas Eve, were endeavoring to make a few pennies selling matches or ribbons or things to eat. Frank and Laurie made a purchase themselves, or rather Frank did—baked potatoes, from the hot-potato man. While they juggled the potatoes from hand to hand, loving the warmth but scarcely able to endure it, Frank spoke of something which had been puzzling him.

"Laurie, what do you think? If your mam walked into your room now, would you be there?"

Laurie had wondered about that himself. "I don't know. I really don't know. I think maybe I would."

"A sort of shell, like? A spirit?"

"Real, I think," said Laurie, hesitant and uncertain.

Frank reached out and tweaked his sleeve. "But you're real *here*. So's Rosie." He was silent for a moment, and then burst out, half angrily, "I can't make end nor side of this!"

"It's a mystery, Frank. There's no knowing it."

At that moment the big man reappeared, so suddenly that there seemed a strong possibility he'd been ejected from the gin palace. Though he was even more staggery than before, he continued north in a way that suggested he had some glimmering of where home was, and meant to get there that night. Laurie and Frank, close on his heels, exchanged exultant glances when he turned into Cavendish Square. Surely they were right. He crossed to the center of the Square and, clutching the garden railings, wished the statue of Lord George Bentinck, 1802-1848, the compliments of the season. Cold and heedless the marble remained, but the servant—it *must* be the servant—appeared to be satisfied, even gratified by his reception, muttering something about his lordship being "very civil," and having "no side." Unlike *some* was the inference.

Laurie thought he would die of impatience and cold while this one-sided meeting was taking place. Even after he'd lost interest in his lordship, the man continued almost hanging on the railings. Laurie suspected he wasn't feeling awfully well, and didn't wonder at it. However the approach of a group of boys from the other end of the Square drew his attention at last. He stared vacantly as they halted outside number sixteen, arranged themselves around one of their number who held a lantern, and launched lustily into "Good Christian Men, Rejoice."

The front door opened and framed in the soft golden glow of the hall stood a woman Laurie immediately thought of as a "comfortable body." Two young girls bobbed behind her.

"Lovely, boys, lovely!" she exclaimed, sounding as though she meant it, when they'd finished their carol. "It's good of you to come just the same, with Master Francis not home. I quite thought we'd be forgotten! Now, give us another, and then you can come inside for your Christmas treat."

Hearing this, Laurie reacted quickly. "Come on,"

he said, pulling the surprised Frank by the arm. They darted heedlessly past their quarry, who in any case took no notice of them, and approached the carolers. "Mingle," ordered Laurie, edging into the group.

The boys struck up "Once in Royal David's City," and Laurie joined in. Frank just stood, looking uncomfortable. "Sing!" hissed Laurie.

"I don't know it," whispered Frank unhappily.

"Then hum."

This poor Frank did, and managed pretty well, apart from a few awkward spots where he anticipated the tune would take a certain course, and hummed in that direction, but the tune went somewhere else; then he had to pretend he'd been harmonizing.

Some of the boys eyed the intruders curiously, and a few looked disapprovingly at Frank's ragged clothes. They were all tidy and cleanly dressed themselves. Laurie liked carols, and sang with great pleasure. In his enthusiasm he forgot he was wearing Master Francis's coat, but in the third verse he remembered, and sank himself deeper into the group, no harm done.

Their song finished, the boys needed no further invitation to come inside, in fact this may have been the whole point of the exercise. They were filing up the steps when, suddenly, the man Laurie and Frank had been following came charging out of the shadows like a bull. Roaring like a bull as well.

"What do you mean, woman, letting them young limbs into the house?" he demanded, swaying a little.

The housekeeper turned in amazement.

"Why, Mr. Questing, it's what Master would want. I couldn't forgive myself—Master wouldn't forgive me —if I turned them away. The lads are all Master Francis's friends, you know, he sings in the choir with them at All Saints'."

The words, quietly but firmly spoken, were so obviously true that even a gin-clouded mind could not deny them. The man stood, baffled, angry, and powerless to intervene, as the boys followed the housekeeper inside, the braver souls among them smirking as they passed him. Laurie and Frank went, too.

They were led into the basement kitchen. The chimney piece and walls had been prettily decorated with wreaths and loops of evergreens and berries, and altogether it was as cheerful and snug a sanctum as you could find, and so warm that within two minutes Laurie's frozen fingers, toes, and nose were tingling pleasurably. The boys crowded around the blazing fire, laughing and joking with the housekeeper, Mrs. Bidgood by name, and plainly a favorite. The two young maids, Flora and Emmy—Laurie was particularly interested to see Emmy—bustled about producing Christmas cake and mince pies and lemonade for all, while Mrs. Bidgood made tea for herself and anyone who wanted it.

It was Christmas, which after all does have a special feel, and Christmas spirit seemed to have infected the boys to the extent that they accepted the strangers in their midst willingly enough for a time, but it was inevitable that questions should be asked. Laurie fended them off by answering, mysteriously, "The vicar knows about us," surprising even himself by the readiness of his lie, and the cunning way it implied that there were special circumstances to the case which the vicar knew but which couldn't be divulged to just anyone. This silenced most of the boys, but one remained unconvinced, and gave it as his opinion that the pair were beggar boys who'd simply seized an opportunity for a feed. If not that then something worse, and he concluded with dark mutterings about counting the spoons after they'd gone.

"Oh, what a doubting Thomas of a Dick. Do be quiet," said a pleasant, open-faced boy Laurie had already been thinking he'd like to know.

"Be quiet yourself, Roger Pickup," retorted Dick. "Look at his clothes," pointing to Frank. "Is that a beggar or a thief? I ask you!"

Frank, who had been beginning to enjoy himself, turned red.

"I'm neither. I earn my living," he said, eyes turned to Mrs. Bidgood, imploring her to believe him.

Laurie was about to jump to his defense when help came from an unexpected quarter.

"Shame on you!" stormed little Emmy, the maid. "Not half an hour since you were singing your heart out about peace and joy and goodwill to men, and I see it was just words with you. Look at him. When do you think he last put himself outside a good dinner? Look at his coat," she said, plucking at the threadbare sleeve through which a thin elbow protruded. "How warm do you think he was this night out in the Square? What matter where he comes from, poor lamb, we should be glad of the chance to be good Samaritans." Shyness caught up with her and she stopped abruptly, turning as red as Frank and clutching nervously at her apron. Laurie felt like cheering and Frank would have died for her from that moment.

Mrs. Bidgood looked astonished, but there was no censure mixed with her astonishment, it was simply that she'd never heard so many words from Emmy before.

"His coat is thin, certainly," she said, raising the sleeve Emmy had just dropped, and giving it a brisk, housewifely examination. "There're those things Mistress put out to go to the orphanage in the cupboard under the stairs. See if you can find something there that might fit him, Emmy dear." She dismissed her with a pat and a smile that seemed to speak approval; very reassuring to the shy girl, only sixteen herself, and experiencing her first Christmas away from home. She was glad of the opportunity to leave the room and collect her thoughts, and only realized long afterward that Mrs. Bidgood had sent her, rather than Flora, for that very reason.

When she returned a few minutes later, it was to see an embarrassed Frank trying on Dick's gloves, which he'd offered in a burst of remorse and Christmas goodwill. The gesture pleased everyone, and the party went forward with increased jollity. Rosie became hot and restless and demanded release, and the boys fell about with mirth to think a cat had gone caroling. Which shows to what a pitch their spirits had risen, since it isn't all that funny. Mrs. Bidgood produced warm milk, and Rosie established herself by the fire as to the manner born. She'd never seen an open fire or a hearth or anything of that nature before, but she'd done a lot of living that night, and felt well able to cope.

Mrs. Bidgood brought out the yule log. She hadn't meant to, it was for tomorrow, but they were all enjoying themselves so much she felt she must. Questing put his head around the door at this stage, but refused an invitation to come in. He scowled and said he had better things to do, and just hoped those danged boys didn't mean to eat them out of house and home, quite. There was a burst of laughter when he disappeared sulkily. Mrs. Bidgood said they oughtn't to laugh at him, but couldn't hide her own smiles.

Someone suggested a song. They had one, then another. Before long Frank was standing on a chair rendering "Duck-legged Dick," flushed and excited in his new blue coat with silver buttons, his new gloves poking out of a pocket.

Laurie saw all this with a heart full of gratitude to Mrs. Bidgood, Emmy, Flora, and the boys of All Saints', wherever All Saints' may have been. It was wonderful to see Frank's acceptance and his obvious happiness. He could have watched him all night. And anyway, it was such a good party, and Mrs. Bidgood's cooking was so marvelous, he would like to have stayed to the end; but while everyone was clapping and cheering Frank's song, and demanding another—he really sang very well—he picked up Rosie, eased by degrees toward the door, and slipped from the pleasant fug of the kitchen into the darkness outside. The chill struck him immediately. He peered anxiously around in case Questing was still lurking about, then padded swiftly up the stairs to the front hall, and up again to the bedroom that was by now growing so familiar. There he lay down with Rosie on top of him, as before, and pulled the quilt over them both. He was tired, very tired, but also overstimulated; he had to unwind before sleep could come. So he thought about the events of the night, a succession of pleasures and shocks, warmth and shivering cold, laughter and fright, that was as far as it could be from his own tame in North Sydney.

There was to be a robbery. They must stop it. At least, he supposed Frank must stop it, being on the spot all the time. He wondered whether it would be possible to get the address of the Pembertons in Devon. They could write to them. Or was the postal system invented yet? Surely it was? Frank must watch the house closely, note anything funny, especially watch for the young man who was to be sent to incriminate Emmy. Emmy. *There* was a girl! Laurie smiled as he reflected that Emmy had done more good than she knew when she spoke up for Frank. If she'd done good for him, she'd done no less for herself. Mrs. Bidgood, he was sure, had a clearer idea of what went on in Emmy's head than she'd had before, and liked what she saw. It would be far harder to convince her now that Emmy could be a party to a crime. But how much influence did Mrs. Bidgood have with the Pembertons? Did Questing have more? They must be pretty dopey people if he did.

He thought about Frank, and smiled again. How happy he'd left him, and he had a new coat and new gloves, and a full stomach, and Mrs. Bidgood would notice him in the future. Laurie had discovered tonight that Frank had very little idea what Christmas was all about, apart from the chance to make extra money. He had been shocked, but a little thought showed him that he ought not to be surprised, considering the life Frank had led. He fell asleep at last with the comfortable thought that, whatever else Frank didn't know, he had learnt something of what Christmas could do to people's hearts this night.

Later, at Christ Church St. Laurence, Mrs. Langridge looked down at Laurie during a hymn, and was very surprised at what she saw. A moment before he had been singing lustily, but now he had stopped, and was standing there looking most peculiar. Was he going to faint? He didn't look pale or sick. Was he simply overcome by the splendor of it all—the color, light, music, crowds? Very likely that was it, and no wonder.

She was right—in fact he'd just decided to be a bishop when he grew up. But that was only part of it. He was also reflecting that this was the second time that night that he'd sung "Once in Royal David's City" and that a different season, a different hemisphere, a different century separated the two occasions. It was enough to silence anyone.

7

After this nothing happened for a time. That is, Laurie's visits continued—and seemed to gain momentum, as they occurred almost every night—but none of Frank's careful watching gained a scrap more information about the robbery. In the meantime, lessons continued, and Frank was an apt pupil. He was bright, and more importantly he wanted to learn, and his delight when letters and then whole words yielded up their mysteries was worth all Laurie's trouble.

Laurie was notorious at the library by then, with his inquiries about everything from teaching methods to the year the penny post was introduced. It came home to him, finally, that he was being something of a nuisance, and he tried to do his research alone. But by then he was a "case," the library staff discussed him hilariously at morning tea, and different ones would come and volunteer help, either because they were genuinely intrigued or because knowledge of a new line of inquiry, the stranger the better, would give them an opportunity to shine in the staffroom. Then Clare joined in. She'd never given a moment's trouble before, but now she was demanding all sorts of information about working-class clothes in the 1860s, and *she* was quite undauntable.

At this time Clare was always muttering about serge, nankeen, drill, stuff, fustian—all, Laurie gathered, fabrics, most of them now unobtainable. She had to decide on suitable substitutes, and, of course, she had to be careful not to use synthetics. Working mainly at Laurie's place, where fewer questions were asked, she adapted a short coat, purchased from a St. Vincent de Paul shop, into a jacket, braided at the edges, with a single button at the neck and a small, turned-down collar, exactly in 1860s fashion. She made a waistcoat in a sort of mud color, hoping that might be what the books meant when they talked of "drab" breeches or "drab" coats. ("It's the drabbest thing I know," she said.) Then she wanted to try a Norfolk suit, though they didn't come in till the late '60s. "He'd be ahead of the fashion," she urged, but Laurie said Frank wouldn't understand, and she gave in in the end.

Laurie said Frank must have a hat, since it never occurred to any Victorian not to. This turned out to be a great success, and made up for Clare's disappointment over the Norfolk suit. It was a cap, really, with a flat, checked cloth crown and a patent leather peak. Laurie felt a bit odd wearing it to bed.

The first thing Frank wanted to learn to write was his name. Laurie wasn't sure how Kilderbee was spelled; it wasn't a name he'd ever seen before. Back home, he looked in the phone book. There was one Kilderbee, quite nearby at Wollstonecraft, and K-I-L-D-E-R-B-E-E was what he taught Frank. He hoped there were no other versions.

One day he found himself in Cavendish Square about midday. It was always the same date as he'd left behind, except for the trifling difference of one hundred and fifteen years, but he never knew what time it was going to be. He was always glad when it was daytime, even though it made it harder to get out the front door unseen. This time, Frank was busy on the crossing, it being a wet, dirty day, the best sort of day in the crossing sweeper line of work. It seemed a pity to make him knock off and lose customers, but Frank was always ready for his next lesson—a pencil and note pad were always in his pocket, in case. This time, the lesson was conducted under the dripping lime trees in the Square, and then they went to a coffeeshop to warm up. Laurie found himself beholden to Frank for yet another cup of coffee, and remembered guiltily that he'd been going to bring back something to sell. He hadn't done so because he always seemed so weighted down with pencils and paper, flannel shirts, caps, and

so on, that he felt silly enough going to bed without clutching a vase or spoons or anything salable as well. What *could* he sell? He looked down at the ball-point pen with which he'd been correcting Frank's exercise, and knew.

They took the pen to a stationer in Paternoster Row, near St. Paul's, where Laurie did the talking, because the story was that this magical pen had been invented by his father in Australia, and that they'd come to England to market it. It was all quite secret as yet, and his father would be furious if he knew, but Laurie had vowed to take home a present from the Old Country for his old granny, and he didn't know how he could except by sacrificing one of his pens. The man was suspicious, but by the boy's voice he could come from the Colonies—he was no Londoner, that was certain— and a demonstration showed that the pen was truly remarkable, and worked on an entirely new principle. Fancy not having to dip it in ink! And what a thing to have it first in all London! Greed and vanity won, and he offered Laurie one pound for it. Frank gasped, and Laurie was learning enough about the times to know that this was a lot of money. He felt bound to say that the pen would not last forever. The man came down to ten shillings at this, and Laurie took it. Next day, according to Frank, it was displayed on a square of red velvet in the shop window, with a note to say it was a miraculous new invention, made from the shining wood of the rare plastic tree, found only in the colony of New South Wales, and was the only one of its kind in the northern hemisphere. The price was two pounds.

"Some mark up!" commented Laurie wryly, and had no compunction in bringing back three more, for which he insisted on getting one pound each. So he made three pounds ten shillings, and gave it all to Frank. A fortune! Frank moved into a different room, in the same tenement, which he didn't share with anyone. He also bought some strong boots, three second-hand books, a nightshirt, a china cat, and two mugs bearing pictures of Queen Victoria. These were for Laurie and Clare, in whom Frank was keenly interested. Laurie sensed the pleasure it gave Frank to give them, and was properly thankful. However, though he clutched them hard on the bed in Cavendish Square, he woke empty-handed in North Sydney, and they were still lying on the quilt next time he crossed the years. There was only one-way traffic, then, from the present to the past and back again, and a half-formed dream of Laurie's, of bringing Frank into the twentieth century, was reluctantly abandoned.

Frank was branching out in other ways. One Sunday he put on his new clothes and went to All Saints', where he saw things that amazed and puzzled him, and where the boys he'd seen in the kitchen in Cavendish

Square, now for some reason all decked out in white dresses, noticed him sitting in a dazed sort of fashion toward the front of the church, and made a fuss of him in the courtyard afterward. Roger Pickup told the vicar that this was the boy he'd told him about, the one who sang like a bird. *Now* did he remember him? Frank froze, remembering Laurie's lie, but the vicar only patted him on the head, said he hoped to hear him sing very soon, and gave him a little copy of the Psalms. Pleased, on the whole, with his expedition, Frank bore his book away and set about reading it.

He didn't expect to find it easy, because he couldn't read very well yet, but he was more confused than even he had anticipated. He even had trouble with the title—he'd been calling it "Palms," and Laurie had to tell him it was "Salms," and it was part of the Bible.

"I thought it didn't seem to have much of a story," said Frank, and Laurie had to hide a smile.

" 'Moab is my washpot; over Edom will I cast out my shoe,' " quoted Frank. "What does that mean, Laurie?"

"I don't know," Laurie had to admit, thinking about it.

"Or this bit. 'Save me from the lion's mouth: Thou hast heard me also from among the horns of the unicorns.' What's a unicorn?"

"It's an animal that doesn't exist. Never did."

"Who's in the horns of the unicorns?"

Laurie hesitated. "God, I think."

"What's He doing in the horns of an animal that doesn't exist?"

"It's poetic language, Frank. It's not meant what we say *literally*."

"What about 'the iniquity of my heels'?"

"What?"

" 'The iniquity of my heels shall compass me about.' I know what iniquity means, I asked Roger Pickup. But what I don't understand is *why* his heels were wicked. What could they have done, ever?"

Laurie laughed outright. "Oh, Frank, I don't know. I'll ask Dad. Leave the Psalms for now. At least the hard ones. Here, I've brought this. It's called *Treasure Island,* and it hasn't been written yet. It's a very famous book. Now come on, we'll try the first chapter. You read, and I'll fill in the words you can't. I think you'll like it."

"Did you find out about the transportation of convicts, Laurie?"

"Yes, it stopped in New South Wales in about 1850, but continued in Western Australia right up to 1868."

"Oh, so I could go there. There's time," said Frank, brightening.

"What do you mean?" asked Laurie.

"I was thinking I might do something. Oh, nothing very bad," Frank hurried on, seeing Laurie's expres-

99

sion, "just enough to get me transported. When this is all over. When I'm older."

"But why, Frank?"

Frank was suddeny shy, and groped for words. "I've got no one here," he said at last. "I just feel I'd like to go to Sydney. The part where you live. And Clare. I'd like to feel that . . . that you were coming after me. That I knew the places you'd know."

Laurie was touched, but there could be no two ways about it for a bishop-to-be! "Don't do anything wrong, Frank. Not for that or anything. You can go to Sydney as a free settler. Lots of people must be doing it."

"But the cost!"

"You'll be able to afford that. When you can read and write well, you'll be able to get a good job. You can save up. What about shorthand? I could get some books about it. Charles Dickens, the famous author, started that way, you know."

"Did he?" Frank hesitated. "Well, I suppose I'm just talking. When it come to the point . . ."

"Came," murmured Laurie absently.

". . . came to the point, I don't suppose I could rob anyone." He grinned. "Anyway, what if they just put me in Newgate prison?"

For Frank, it was a good time, of learning, discovery, the consolidation of one friendship and the beginning of others—with Roger Pickup, Mrs. Bidgood, Emmy—that were as far from the teeming, ugly world of the tenements, which was all he had ever known,

100

as they could be. He had always been lonely, an out-
sider; and though he had been proud, sure that he was
different and would climb out of the slums somehow,
there had been moments when his courage failed,
when he looked at the hopeless people around him and
wondered which of them had once been "different,"
too. He couldn't be the first. Now he felt more hopeful
than he'd ever been. He was on the way!

Then one Thursday afternoon in mid-January,
Frank saw Emmy walking out with a man he immediately knew to be the quiet man's "young friend." It
had started then. He was so struck, so concerned for
Emmy, that he stood stock still in the middle of the
road and was almost run over by a hackney coach.

Surely Emmy wouldn't be taken in! She was too
nice a girl, her head was on straight. The man was
handsome—very—but she would see he was just too
well-dressed, too much at ease, too attentive.

It was an anxious afternoon for Frank, and he was
always pausing in his sweeping to watch for Emmy's
return. He was watching, too, for Laurie. He never
knew when he was coming. How good it would be if
he just happened along now! But he didn't, and Frank
formed his plans alone.

Emmy returned, still escorted by the young man,
about six. Was it Frank's imagination—because he

wanted it to be so—or was her good-bye perfunctory, her smile strained and tight? She certainly wasted no time getting indoors.

When the door closed the young man remained on the top step for a moment, smiling to himself. Then he pulled out his watch, held it toward the portico light, repocketed it, and set off briskly down the street. Frank followed him.

On a hot, airless night in Sydney, Mrs. Langridge was lying awake, trying to remember the name of the little fair girl who sat next to her in class 3A in 1942—she went to ballet classes, she remembered, at the *other* ballet school in town—when she thought she heard Laurie cry out. Rising immediately, she hurried up the stairs to his room. He was asleep, but tossing restlessly, and no wonder. Though he was covered by the sheet, she could see that he was wearing his duffle coat. Also, there was a hard-looking hump at the end of the bed that had to be more than feet. She lifted the sheet and saw that he was wearing wool socks and his school shoes, and that both feet were tucked into a plastic dry-cleaning bag, presumably to save the sheets.

As she stared, aghast, he rolled again and a copy of *Pitman's Shorthand* slipped out from a fold of the coat; also two ball-point pens. Uttering a little cry of distress Mrs. Langridge ran down the stairs to wake her husband. Perhaps it's just as well she decided against waking Laurie, since he may not have been there. On the other hand he may, there's no telling.

When Mr. Langridge had assured himself, by his own visit to the attic, that his wife had not been dreaming, they sat down to discuss the matter, both considerably shaken. They had tried to be good parents, and Laurie had seemed to be shaping well.

"He's always been a dreamy boy, but sensible . . . fairly. Hasn't he?" whispered Mrs. Langridge anxiously.

"I thought so," replied Mr. Langridge, squeezing his wife's hand comfortingly.

They were silent.

"You know," continued Mrs. Langridge finally, "I'm not sure that that Clare is a good influence. Perhaps she's to blame."

"Why? She seems a nice little thing."

"Yes, but she's . . . an unusual child. Her great passion is Victorian costume, you know."

"Really? How interesting," said her husband, showing signs of brightening. "Fascinating subject, costume. Fascinating."

"Yes," said Mrs. Langridge hurriedly, before he could go off on a tangent, "but don't you think it's, well, odd, for a child of eleven or twelve?"

"Not at all," replied Mr. Langridge, halting Mrs.

Langridge's train of thought just like that. She thought then of her own twelve-year-old self—the beetles, the woodwork, the obsession with Ancient Egypt.

"No, I suppose not," she agreed, with a small, rueful grin. "Well, what then?"

"Do you suppose," began Mr. Langridge thoughtfully, "that Tom and Helen are right, and we should have *made* him run around playing football and joining the Police Boys' Club and riding surfboards and that sort of thing all these years?"

"I don't know. I don't *know*," Mrs. Langridge almost whimpered.

Another pause. Then, "We could try it, I suppose" came from both at once, and they were too worried to make the usual joke about great minds, and so on.

Thus it was that Laurie was shocked to be informed next morning that his father had a bit of unexpected leave, and he thought it would be nice if they all went up to Umina to see Auntie Helen and Uncle Tom and the boys.

"No," he almost shouted. "We only just saw them Boxing Day. What do we want to see them again for?"

His parents exchanged brief glances. Keep calm, the glances said.

"Well, dear, it *is* the summer holidays, and there's the beach at Umina, and Sandy and Steve to play with. It's not much fun for you here."

"Yes it is," he asserted distractedly, striding up and

down, unaware that every sign of agitation was sealing his fate by convincing his parents that action was urgently needed.

They packed up the car and went that very day, and there was nothing Laurie could do about it.

Frank wondered where Laurie was. Two days went by, three, four, and Frank needed him. Surely the magic wasn't going to end now? He needed him so badly.

On that Thursday evening he'd followed the handsome young man to the heart of Seven Dials, a rookery where even the police wouldn't venture except in groups. Tracking wasn't easy in the mean, ill-lit passages and lanes, hampered by the residents—pale, stunted children, surly women, vicious-looking men—who'd overflowed from crowded, stale rooms on to the scarcely less stale streets. Frank was ragged enough (not having his "good" clothes on) to pass for one of themselves, so he wasn't physically molested, but he did lose his new cap, tweaked from his head by an unknown hand. He couldn't stop to give chase, and it would have been the worse for him if he had. The pursuit ended in a squalid beershop where Frank saw his man pause and then approach someone sitting alone at the end of a long table. The quiet man? Frank suspected it was, and what he overheard confirmed his

suspicions. Fortunately, they made no attempt to keep their conversation to themselves. There was no need —the place was a regular thieves' kitchen, nearly everyone there was "in the trade." Frank bought himself some ale, and tried to look like a young pickpocket, cocky and sharp, out to impress the older, more experienced thieves. He knew their style well enough, having seen them, even shared beds with them, in the low lodging houses in which he'd occasionally passed a night. "Padding kens," the boys called them, or "bug traps." The type was not uncommon, too, in Catherine Wheel Alley.

He didn't like the ale—that part of the act wasn't easy—but he must have been convincing on the whole. No one questioned him, and he learned a lot. The robbery was to be on the Friday of the following week, three days before the Pembertons were due home. The goods—china, silverware, pictures, and furnishings— were to be loaded onto a cart in the dead of night via the front door. No locks would be forced. Suspicion would fall on the girl.

"How did you get on? Is she fly?" inquired the older man.

"She don't suspect a thing. She's hooked proper," returned the handsome youth, laughing and preening in a very repellent way—or so it seemed to Frank.

Had she been "fly," wondered Frank, as he zigzagged around trying to find his way out of the rookery, stumbling up blind alleys, slipping on rough and sometimes slimy cobbles, feeling always that he was being watched from the hard, insolent stares of those who belonged in that ugly and threatening place. Surely she could see through him! What was Emmy, to be swayed by a lot of black curls, a big white smile, and a pearl pin, probably stolen?

Clare was a biddable child, nicely brought up by a nice mother and a nice father and a rather fierce (but nice) grandmother. They were all sure she was very clever and was going to do great things and make them very proud when she grew up, and she thought so too, on the whole, so they got along very nicely together. That's why it felt so unreal, what she did. It was like a dream, sneaking out of the house at eleven o'clock at night, wearing a long dress and a shawl and carrying a stepstool.

It was fortunate that she knew about the pantry window, and she just hoped that, since the Langridges had gone away in a rush, there hadn't been time to have it fixed. It was rather high, but she was ready for that. Mounting the stepstool, she rattled and pulled and heaved at the window, and it gave. With a sigh of relief, and a flutter of fright too, because now she was committed, she pushed the window up and climbed in among Mrs. Langridge's jars of strawberry and pineapple jam. All the time it was as though someone else was doing it. Clare Elliot didn't *do* things like this!

In the darkness she felt her way to the stairs, and went up toward Laurie's room. The empty house felt watchful; the air was thick and oppressive. Creaks and squeaks from here and there seemed to have a protesting note, as though doors and stairs and floorboards were grumbling to one another about the intruder. An intruder was what she certainly felt like, and a frightened one. In Laurie's room she hurriedly rubbed her way around the bedknobs and then was glad to leap into bed and pull the covers up, despite the warmth of the night. She lay there trembling. What if someone came? What if someone had seen her break in—because that's what she'd done—and had called the police? What would she say? They couldn't charge her with breaking and entering. She'd entered, yes, but she hadn't broken; nor had she stolen. She'd just gone to bed, which would sound so silly if she were found out. With these thoughts to distract her, a sleepless night seemed likely, but Clare was a determined girl and she'd come to sleep. She lay on her back in the yoga dead-man's pose, which she'd seen on TV, and breathed slowly and steadily, blanking out her mind and pretending she was lying on a cloud, sinking into its soft, woolly depths. She slept.

Naturally she hoped to wake in Cavendish Square, but she didn't count on it by any means. She had rubbed the bedknobs just as Laurie had described but

110

maybe the magic was only for him. Even if it weren't, it didn't work every night, though it seemed to have been at its height in the last few weeks.

Well, it did work. She woke, shivered, wondered and hoped, leaped out of bed and to the window, and saw London. It was dark but coming light; a few last stars were fading in what promised to be a clear, hard sky. Down below in the Square, figures were moving around. Was Frank one of them? She wrapped her shawl around her shoulders, tiptoed to the door and paused, listening. She couldn't get caught now, that would be too awful. Like Laurie on another occasion, she breathed a prayer of thankfulness for the absent family, then crept into the hall and down the stairs. In the front hall she could hear sounds down below; probably the servants at breakfast. Just as she was about to open the front door, it rang. Her heart skipped a beat, and she stood panic-stricken. Then she heard footsteps coming up from downstairs, and a grumbling voice complaining about callers at this hour. Jerked into action, she opened the door and shut it quickly behind her. The caller, surprised at the quick response to his ring, begged pardon for calling at the front door, but they hadn't seemed to hear his knock down below, and asked whether there were any knives to grind, or scissors to mend. "I couldn't say, I'm sure. It's my day off," gabbled Clare, and fled down the street.

She studied the faces of people she passed. The

111

clothes were different, but the faces were the same—anxious, sad, cheerful, smug, stupid, mean, patient, all the rest—just as though they came from Sydney, 1978. No one took any notice of her. What would they think if they knew?

She walked up and down, to keep warm, and made several short sorties out of the Square, but she didn't want to go far. It was about an hour before Frank came. She saw him advancing from Margaret Street, carrying his broom. She would have known him even without the broom—the alert set of his head, the quirk at the corner of his mouth, the straight glance were all that she had imagined.

"Frank Kilderbee, I presume," she said, going toward him. She couldn't resist it.

Frank was astonished and delighted when he understood this latest turn of events. He had been interested in Clare for some time, and they had sent innumerable messages to each other through Laurie, so it didn't feel like a meeting of strangers at all. They were friends.

"The clothes are fine. Thank you so much. Look at this," chattered Frank excitedly, capering about and waving his arms—and broom—to demonstrate the snug fit of the coat Clare had provided. Maybe he became a little overexcited for a time. It was relief, really. He'd been very much afraid the magic had ended, since it had been five anxious days since he'd seen Laurie. He'd missed him very much since they were truly friends, but he'd also missed Laurie's advice and

112

help at this time when things were coming to a head. Clare explained what had happened, and, in spite of everything, Frank couldn't help smiling at the idea of Laurie dumbly resisting all his parents' attempts to discover why he had gone to bed in winter clothes on the hottest night of the summer.

Calming down, he confided to Clare what he had overheard in Seven Dials, and said he'd been nearly frantic thinking what to do. He wished he could contact the Pembertons, but he didn't know their whereabouts, beyond the fact that they were in Devon. He supposed he'd have to tell the police, but would they listen to him? He had no proof. And would they believe in Emmy's innocence? And what if the date of the robbery was changed? He might be in trouble with the law himself if they thought he was stringing them along.

Clare eyed Lord George Bentinck, frozen in his cold stone. "It *would* be best to let the Pembertons know," she reflected.

"Yes. But how?"

"Do you ever run messages for, what's her name, Mrs. Goodbid?"

"Bidgood. Sometimes."

"Take the mail, maybe?"

"No, never that."

"Oh, too bad. I thought there might be things directed to them in Devon." She paused. "Could you *ask* her then?"

"I'd have to have a reason."

"Yes," agreed Clare thoughtfully. "Could you say you were inquiring about a job? A situation?" she corrected herself, thinking "job" sounded too modern.

"She'd only say they'll be back soon, wait till then."

"So that's out. Well, then."

But now Frank was also thinking along these lines.

"I could say the vicar of All Saints' had asked me to inquire, as there's something he wants to send. Or no, something he particklar wants them to bring back from Devon," he finished, flushed with the brilliance of this latter thought.

"That's very good, Frank."

"Well, you started it, really. About asking and that."

"And I hope you won't mind my saying the word is 'particularly.' I wouldn't mention it only I know you like to know."

"Particularly," he repeated carefully, not feeling nearly as hot and prickly as he usually did when he made mistakes.

So that's what he did. He rang the bell, asked for Mrs. Bidgood, and lied, not quite as professionally as Laurie would have. Mrs. Bidgood, good soul, didn't suspect a thing.

He and Clare discussed the contents of the letter on the crossing. Sometimes Frank swept, and sometimes Clare, who wanted to try it, too. She'd made twopence halfpenny before Frank declared a holiday.

114

"You should see a bit," he explained earnestly. "You won't be back again, I don't suppose."

"I'm coming when I'm grown up."

"And I'll be long dead then," commented Frank ruefully.

They gazed at each other, reflecting on the oddness of things.

9

Well, where would you like to go? There's all London," Frank offered grandly, with a brisk return to safe, everyday things.

Where? There were so many possibilities. Clare thought of Buckingham Palace. She might see the queen. But did she want to? In photos, Queen Victoria always looked like such a grump and a frump. It would be interesting to step up to her and say, "Good morning, Your Majesty. I saw your great-great-granddaughter and your great-great-great-granddaughter a few years ago, and they were looking well," but she was almost certain the queen would not be amused. What then? If it were Sunday, she could go to Hyde Park, stand on a box, and start the ball rolling for Women's Rights. But it was Monday.

She decided on Westminster Abbey, a park, and the river, and everything in between she would leave to Frank; he would enjoy thinking for her. Two minutes after setting off, she added another thing—she wanted to ride in a horse bus.

"It's all right about the fares, Frank, I've brought two more ball-point pens. One writes in green and one in red."

"Fancy! It seems unnatural somehow."

He led her down through St. James's to the Park, where they fed the birds that were there for the winter. Clare wondered whether their infinitely great-great descendants still lived there. She hoped so. She told Frank what she had recently learned herself, that St. James's Park was laid out by a king, the piratical-looking Charles II, who used to walk there with his dogs. Occasionally a dog was stolen, since professional dog stealers could expect a good ransom for the king's pets. Once he advertised in the paper for a missing dog, describing it as "full of blue spots." A nice way of putting it, and a nice, ordinary thing for a king to do. Whenever Clare saw a picture of him now, bejewelled and splendid in flowing black wig, velvet, lace and plumes, she thought of a man advertising for his lost spaniel.

They stood on the bridge over the lake in the Park, and looked one way to the turrets and domes of Whitehall and the other way to the Palace. Then came the Abbey. Frank had never been there before; it was a first for him, too. They prowled around for ages. Clare was disturbed by all the pompous statues and memorials of statesmen and warriors and aristocrats. She hadn't expected that. But she loved the vivid glass, the chapels, the stiff, golden effigies of kings and queens, the tucked-away nooks and corners where the magic was strongest. There was one tiny chapel, the entrance to which, low and leaning, was roofed with gold stars on a blue background. Clare stood there and felt the centuries strong about her.

Clare told Frank that in 1965 the Abbey would be nine hundred years old, and that her aunt had been there at the time (funny how she had to mix her tenses in this mad situation!) and Aunt Margery had said the Abbey was glorious for its birthday, its altars glowing with gold leaf, its chapels bright with color. There had been a war, Clare said, and terrible damage to London, but very little to the Abbey. There was a little hole in an outer wall. You could see daylight through it, and they'd left it there, so they'd never forget how lucky they'd been. Frank was fascinated.

They walked along Whitehall to Trafalgar Square, and saw the National Gallery. Clare looked at its thin, domed tower, and asked Frank if he'd ever heard it referred to as the National Pepperpot, but he never had. Clare's Aunt Margery had.

They climbed the curving steps to the top of a horse bus, squeezed on to a seat, and were carried along the Strand to the City, the one-square-mile heart of London. Progress was slow, since there seemed to be no rules about keeping to the left, or anything like that—just a crush of buses, hansoms, lumbering growlers' carriages and carts, all making their way as best they could. Under these circumstances it was hardly surprising that London smelled of horses! At the Bank of England they got off, went to a stationer, and sold the ball-point pens for one pound each, Clare doing Laurie's part, in which she'd been coached by Frank as they came along. Then they went to a chophouse in a little cobbled court off Lombard Street.

The chophouse, an ancient, crazily-leaning establishment with black, smoky beams, was crowded with the sort of high-backed booths that would by then have been quite familiar to Laurie. It was full of smart, coming-up-in-the-world clerks, all talking at the top of their voices, waving forks in the air to emphasize a point, enjoying themselves hugely. A few looked with impersonal curiosity at Frank and Clare as they stood uncertainly waiting to be shown a place. The waiter was uncertain, too, and Frank, seeing this, made a great point of transferring his money from one pocket to another, dropping one half crown after another into his breast pocket in an apparently absent-minded fashion. The waiter's eyes widened, and he led them to a booth quite near the fire.

They had steak and kidney pudding with baked potatoes and peas, and Clare felt as though she should be downing ale with it, like all the men. Then they had treacle tart. They drank two cups of tea each, and became as uproarious as the clerks. Clare threw back her shawl, and wondered whether her face was as red as Frank's. They had some more treacle tart. A man at a nearby table, amused at seeing such a young pair dining out, sent over two glasses of mulled wine. He

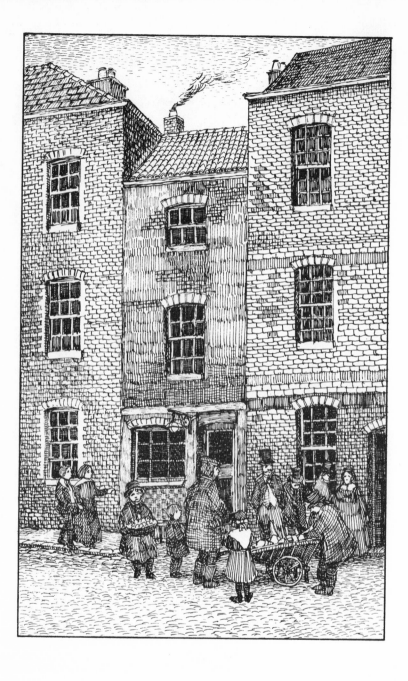

smiled and raised his glass to them when the waiter pointed him out. Clare smiled back doubtfully, and raised her glass to him. She took a mouthful and didn't like it much, though she thought that if she hadn't already been burning up with heat it would have set up a nice glow inside her. Frank didn't much relish his either, apparently, and when the man's attention had drifted back to his companions, they poured the remains of the two glasses into the teapot, giggling conspiratorially. Frank poured out some of this odd mixture and took a mouthful, pulling a most hideous face, which made Clare laugh till she hurt. Laurie wouldn't have recognized her.

The bill was six and twopence, an enormous sum. Frank looked scared for a moment, but recovered in time to pay up as though he did this sort of thing every day. They rolled out to the street feeling about thirty pounds heavier, blinking in the bright, cold sunlight.

Next, the river, and London Bridge wasn't far away. They approached it via Billingsgate, still smelling fishy but with the bustle of the market long over. Frank pointed out Rodway's, where he had first eaten with Laurie. They had a quick look in the church of St. Magnus the Martyr, because Clare liked the name, but it was dark and musty and strange. From the bridge, Clare saw a forest of masts and rigging, an incredible tangle. How it was ever sorted out she couldn't imagine. She stared at the Pool of London and wondered what was wrong, and it was some time before she realized that in her aunt's slides Tower Bridge was there. It couldn't be built yet! Along the gray, muddy shore, mudlarks were wading, searching for lumps of coal, or bits of rope, or anything they could sell. The youngest looked seven or eight, and this was their life. Clare didn't like to think how cold that water must be.

Her tour was completed, to her entire satisfaction, but now Frank added one last item—he wanted a photograph of them together. They walked back to Fleet Street, and turned in at a photographer's. It was a funny business. They had to go out the back to the yard, sit in front of a painted background full of columns and drapes, and do their best to become statues. Frank was nervous—he'd never had his "likeness," as he called it, taken before. Smiles were out of the question; they would turn into desperate grimaces before the thing was over. All Clare could do was try not to look as though she was about to burst into tears, an expression she'd often noticed on people in old photos. It was done at last, and Frank paid his shilling. "No extra charge for two sitters," said the man blandly, and Frank seemed to think this was a great thing, as surely more "power" was needed to photograph two people at once.

When they returned to the street Frank was trying not to swagger, but he was feeling like a bit of a swell. By jingo, the things he did these days!

The outing was over now, both felt it. It only remained to head back to Cavendish Square, which they did, walking more slowly the nearer they approached, and talking constantly all the time. So much to talk about, so little time.

They had to watch for some time, lurking behind Lord George Bentinck, for an opportunity for Clare to get back into the house. They were becoming desperate—and frozen—when Mrs. Bidgood suddenly appeared at the door, looking up and down the Square. Frank squeezed Clare's hand and popped out from behind the statue.

"Oh, Frank dear, I was looking for you," called Mrs. Bidgood, pleased. Frank stopped short a little way from the house, forcing her to come toward him, which she did, very obligingly.

"I was thinking, if you haven't already seen the vicar, would you mind taking him some of my lemon curd tarts when you go? He's that fond of them, and I thought as you were going . . . if you haven't been . . ."

"I haven't been," said Frank, edging around so that his back was toward Clare, and gesturing toward the house with both hands clasped behind him. "And I'm glad to see you, because I'm not quite sure of that address. Bovey Tracy, isn't it?"

"That's right. A funny name, I always think."

"It *is* a funny name, isn't it? How would it be spelled, then?"

"B-O-V-E-Y, first word, T-R-A-C-Y, second word. It's in Devon, mind."

"Oh yes, I was sure of that part." Frank's inquiry was genuine, not just something invented on the spot; Clare had been able to tell him how to spell "Pemberton," but she'd never heard of "Bovey Tracy."

While this exchange was proceeding, Clare softly advanced toward the entrance, and hurried up the steps. In the doorway she paused and looked back over her shoulder. The only acknowledgment Frank could make was a look, over Mrs. Bidgood's shoulder, and it had to be a fairly blank look at that, so as not to attract attention. So they didn't even say good-bye, and maybe that was just as well, since it would have been difficult and sad.

Frank wrote his letter as soon as he got home. It read:

Dear Sir,

I am your freind. Your house will be robed on next fry day. Please come quick. I am the sweaper in the square. Come to me and I will tell you what I know. Qesting is one of them do not trust him.

Your freind,
Frank Kilderbee

It was the best he could do. He hoped it was all right.

10

Laurie and his parents spent a not-very-comfortable time in Umina. It was downright embarrassing to witness Mr. Langridge's attempts at gamboling on the beach with the boys, in his earnest endeavor to be a chum to his son, and Laurie's gamboling wasn't much more successful. Frank and Cavendish Square were very much on his mind, and when he did succeed in switching his mind back to the twentieth century it was usually to see Steve shoving Sandy or Sandy shoving Steve, or hear Steve yelling you-did-you-did-you-did or Sandy yelling didn't-didn't-didn't. That was how they went on all the time, and Laurie couldn't really think his parents wanted him to be like that. Steve had once read a book called *Let's Visit a Cement Plant,* which was "all right," but as far as Laurie could gather, Sandy had never read anything at all.

125

Rosie, bless her, saved the situation at last, thereby dissolving Laurie's last remaining scrap of coolness toward her for what she'd put him through at the circus. It happened this way. Aunt Helen and Uncle Tom owned two dogs, a Great Dane and a small terrier. The trouble was not with the Great Dane—Hamlet was a dog of immense size and immense dignity, who stalked through life looking noble and distant and above earthly considerations—but with Cheeky, the terrier. Cheeky had a chip on his shoulder, perhaps because of his awful name, but more likely because Hamlet's enormous size, compared with his own, gave him very pronounced inferiority feelings. Whereas Hamlet scarcely seemed aware that a cat had come to stay, Cheeky hardly thought of anything else. Rosie was not a big cat, and Cheeky was so delighted to discover an animal even smaller than himself that he devoted all his energies to terrorizing her. Poor Rosie was harassed, pounced on, chased, and yapped at till she almost became a nervous wreck. They tried keeping Rosie in and Cheeky out, but there was a crisis every time someone opened the back door. Cheeky would be lurking outside waiting to scuttle in, and his nails would clatter on the wooden floors as he searched, mad-eyed and excited, for the Enemy. Rosie took to living under the bed on the glassed-in veranda, and an expedition had to be mounted to woo, coax, or drag her out every time they wanted to feed her. Not that she'd eat much.

On the sixth day Mr. Langridge cracked. He said he couldn't bear Rosie's imploring looks any longer, and they would have to go. Laurie almost cheered. They loaded up the car and left after lunch, with much relief to all the Langridges, though none of them admitted it out loud. Only Rosie looked triumphant, striding up and down the ledge behind the back seat and lashing her tail at Cheeky outside. Cheeky looked miserable; you could almost feel sorry for him. Back to keeping out from under Hamlet's paws!

Laurie wanted to go to London so much that night that he was sure he wouldn't. He felt so tensed up and anxious when he rubbed the bedknobs that he didn't see how the magic could possibly penetrate into him. He forgot the magic wasn't in him at all, but in the bed, and the bed wasn't the least bit anxious. He woke in Cavendish Square, to a gray, louring day and gusty wind rattling the panes. He had to dress in Master Pemberton's clothes again, since he'd gone to bed blameless in yellow cotton pajamas, in case his mother came snooping.

The reunion with Frank, in the middle of Holles Street, nearly resulted in their both being run over by a hansom cab. They were so delighted that anyone would have thought they'd been separated for years. Well, that's what it had felt like.

There was a great deal to be told, especially on Frank's side. Laurie was amazed to hear about Clare—

there hadn't been time to see her that afternoon—and there was what Frank had overheard in Seven Dials, and Emmy, and the letter.

"So the robbery's tonight?"

"Yes. Or in the early hours of the morning, more like. What are we going to do?"

"I suppose we must tell the police, as there's been no word from Mr. Pemberton. Are you sure you got his address right?"

"I'm sure."

"What about warning Mrs. Bidgood?"

"What could she do? It would only frighten her. Might even put her in danger."

They stood irresolute, buffeted by gusts of windy rain. Frank made a few half-hearted swipes with his broom, as though it helped him to think. It was while they stood thus that a slight figure drifted out of the gloom, seemingly from nowhere, and a correspondingly light voice said, "Pardon me, but I'm looking for Frank Kilderbee. Are either of you . . ."

"That's me" and "That's him," said Frank and Laurie together.

"Oh. How do you do? My name is . . ."

"Pemberton!" finished both boys excitedly.

Now, how much to be said! The boys started in right there in the road, but it wasn't very successful, what with the weather and the traffic and Frank's calls to business. Besides, Mr. Pemberton shouldn't be seen. When Laurie pointed this out, Mr. Pemberton

128

looked helpless for a moment and then suggested they might like a spot of tea, if they hadn't already . . . He'd come straight from the train and was a bit . . . He seemed to have trouble finishing sentences.

He took them to a quiet tearoom, plain but warm and dry, and there they ate brown bread and butter, scones and jam, and some things called maids-of-honor, and drank lots of good hot tea, while they talked and talked. The boys talked, that is. Mr. Pemberton listened, for the most part, drawing patterns on the tablecloth with the tip of his knife and looking sadder and more hangdog as the tale progressed. At the end, they sat back and looked at him expectantly. This seemed to embarrass him and he wriggled inside his clothes in a most peculiar way and cleared his throat several times.

"Well?" said Laurie, becoming impatient.

"The thing is . . . why should I believe you?" Mr. Pemberton colored, and looked as though he felt he'd said something in terribly bad taste. Seeing Frank pale and Laurie turn red with anger, he hurried on, "I'm sorry, but really I must mention . . . You see, I don't know you at all. This could be some elaborate hoax, or something more sinister. You could be criminals yourselves. Isn't it so?" His eyes appealed to them to consider his point of view. There was something boyish and helpless about him that was quite engaging, but Laurie refused to let his anger cool.

"What kind of hoax, for goodness' sake? There's

nothing in this for us—only trouble. And danger. Would *you* go to Seven Dials at night? Well, we've done what we can. We've warned you. Come on, Frank."

He half arose, and Frank gazed anxiously from one to the other. Then Mr. Pemberton waved him down again, making worried noises in his throat that may have been real English words, but certainly didn't sound like it.

"Wait. I didn't say I *didn't* believe you. That's just it. I should be suspicious—my brother-in-law would, I'm sure—but . . ." His brow wrinkled, you could see him thinking not absolutely kind thoughts of this brother-in-law. "The odd thing is, you know, that I *think* I believe you. Though why I should . . . You're only lads, poor ones at that. Crossing sweepers! And your clothes . . ." He peered at them as though he were a little shortsighted, and Laurie, remembering he was wearing Master Pemberton's clothes, sat down quickly. A further interval of thought followed, then, "Yes, I *do* believe you!" Mr. Pemberton concluded, firm and certain at last.

"Thank goodness!" Frank's tone was heartfelt, and the grin that followed one of his broadest. Mr. Pemberton smiled back; you could tell he considered himself quite something for being so strong and decisive. If his brother-in-law could see him now!

"I shall inform the police," he announced importantly, "and I'd be obliged if you would accompany

130

me. We shall lay all our information before them."

On the way he told them, confidentially, "I never liked Questing, you know. I wouldn't have appointed him only he came recommended by my wife's brother and he would have thought it so . . . But if I'd had my way . . ."

The police were bound to pay attention to a man as well-dressed and well-connected as Mr. Pemberton (his brother-in-law, it turned out, was a baronet) even though he was not, in appearance and manner, impressive himself. It is difficult to say whether Laurie and Frank would have had such a good hearing alone, or perhaps *any* hearing. Everyone had to supply full names and addresses, and when his turn came Laurie instantly gave his address as Clerkenwell (it was a name he'd seen on a horse bus) and invented a street and house number. Sometimes this facility of his for lying worried him.

It was settled that three policemen would arrive in the Square before midnight, and wait out the hours of darkness. Mr. Pemberton wanted to be in the party, and was keen that Laurie and Frank should be present, too, if they wanted to be. The police took kindly to this idea, but perhaps they only wanted to have the boys on hand in case nothing happened, at which time, no doubt, a more serious investigation of *them* would take place. Frank was very keen to be there, and Laurie too, in a way, but for him there were complications which only Frank could know about.

131

To stay would mean spending a much longer time than ever before in the nineteenth century. He'd arrived at about two P.M. Supposing the robbery took place at one A.M., he probably couldn't get away before two, which would make twelve hours—and it could be much later. His previous longest stay had been about five hours, though from what he could gather, Clare must have stayed longer. Of course, it made no difference when he got home, no time had ever passed, but his visits to the nineteenth century had always been just that—visits—with his real life going on in its rightful time and place. The prospect of actually living for a time in this other world made him, quite suddenly, very conscious that he didn't belong. It made him a bit apprehensive, too, in case it was putting too much of a strain on the magic—if that were possible. A problem. Nevertheless, the desire to see what happened was irresistible, and he stayed.

They passed the time—he and Frank—with Mr. Pemberton; he insisted on it. He took them to the Lord Nelson Music Hall, and afterward to supper, smilingly inviting them to "play a good knife and fork." Then, near midnight, they caught a cab to Wimpole Street, and walked from there to Cavendish Square, in order to arrive quietly and inconspicuously.

The rendezvous was a house on the north side of the Square, the owner of which was known to be away, and the servants with him. From here they had a good view of the Pemberton house on the eastern side. They waited down in the area, and the policemen took turns as lookout, sitting or standing on the area steps, eyes just above street level. The rest remained below, crouched against the wall, and only speaking in whispers. It was an unspeakably miserable vigil. The wind had dropped, but the rain persisted, and it was dank and cold in the area. The policemen at least had oilskins; the other three just got wetter and wetter, despite Mr. Pemberton's umbrella, under which they took turns. The doubts and anxieties of all waiting times set in, heightened by the grim conditions of this particular wait. Was it the right night? Had there been a change of plan? Had they heard right? At such times one is capable of doubting almost anything.

One o'clock came, two o'clock, three o'clock. Laurie could hardly remember a time when he *hadn't* been standing in that dripping area, and he was sure he was coming down with the flu. Here was an interesting problem. Supposing he ever got home again, could he wake up with the flu caught a century before? It was a Nice Point, as his father would have said.

Not long after three, a covered cart turned slowly into the Square from Margaret Street. It was a silent operation, the sound of hooves and wheels deadened by the rain. The cart halted outside the Pemberton house, and three men climbed down.

The watching policeman had given the signal that something was up. He was joined by his two col-

133

leagues, while Laurie, Frank, and Mr. Pemberton agonized behind them, trying to edge up the steps for a view. In one snatched glance over a policeman's shoulder, Laurie saw the front door open and a strip of light appear. A figure bulked in the doorway, and by the outline it could only be Questing. Laurie heard Mr. Pemberton draw in his breath. One man remained by the horse and the others hurried up the steps into the house, silent and purposeful. It was too dark and the rain was too heavy to recognize them.

"Aren't you going after them?" Mr. Pemberton almost squeaked.

"Don't worry, sir, they're coopered. Just let them load up and damn themselves good and proper. It'll be the worse for them and the better for us."

"But that's Grandfather Pemberton's clock," Mr. Pemberton whispered, wild-eyed, as the two men stuffed their first pickings into the back of the cart. They returned to the house. From what the watchers could see, Questing handed things and held the door, but took no other part in the proceedings. They watched through two more trips to the cart, and then the constable announced calmly, "Now."

The three policemen surged up the steps into the Square, Mr. Pemberton behind them. The constable paused to call sharply over his sholuder, "Keep back!" and Mr. Pemberton pulled up, looking foolish and uncertain for a moment, till he decided it was probably the boys who were to stay. Then he kept on to-

134

ward his house, in a hesitant, am-I-allowed sort of way, in case the constable *had* meant him as well.

Frank and Laurie watched as the police tackled the thieves, who were plainly taken completely unawares. Questing's first reaction was to slam the door shut, only to reopen it seconds later as he realized his best chance lay in fleeing. He scuttled down the steps and started toward the corner, with a heavy, bearlike roll. The man holding the horse put up no resistance at all, but the other two did. With one policeman chasing Questing, and another securing the cart driver, only one was left to deal with these two, and he seemed to be getting the worst of it. That is, till Mr. Pemberton saw one of the men drag something off the cart and bring it crashing down on the policeman's head.

"Grandfather Pemberton's clock!" he cried, leaping up and down in a very odd way (so that's what "hopping mad" means, thought Laurie) before hurling himself forward, waving his umbrella wildly. More by accident than anything, the heavy handle of the umbrella made contact with the clock-wielding man's head at about the fourth swing, and so dazed him that he became an easy mark for the policeman who had himself been stunned. While he and Mr. Pemberton concentrated on this man, the taller and probably younger of the men saw his chance and sprinted away. Toward Laurie and Frank, as it happened. Without exchanging a word or even a glance, both boys leaped forward when the man was even with them. Laurie

135

brought off a football tackle that would have astounded Sandy and Steve, and Frank somehow pinioned the man's arms behind his back, and sat on him to keep him down. Even so he fought, hunching and bucking his body in an effort to dislodge Frank. Laurie held on to his feet, even after he'd received a nasty kick in the jaw, but it was hard going and the man might eventually have bested them—he was very strong—if the policeman who'd chased Questing hadn't just then come running up. With his help the man was soon secured, and Laurie stood up, nursing his jaw and soaked with mud and rain. He felt rather sick.

Perhaps never again would such an entirely satisfactory time occur to Mr. Pemberton, Laurie, and Frank, as occurred in Mr. Pemberton's drawing room not much later.

For a time the three felt justified in living in the glow of their adventure. Soon, normality would take over—Laurie would be facing a new school, Frank would be on his crossing, Mr. Pemberton would be embroiled with business and family concerns. Soon— but just for the present they laughed and talked and retold the story over and over again for Mrs. Bidgood and Emmy and Flora, who fussed and presented tea and toast and admired in a very gratifying way.

Each, privately, could hardly believe he'd done what

he had done, especially Mr. Pemberton, who could only just restrain himself from driving off to Hyde Park Gate to tell his brother-in-law, who might be a baronet and very tall and commanding, but who had certainly never captured a burglar in his life.

The constable came back about an hour after he and his men had gone off with their captives. He was hailed as an old friend by a boyishly overexcited Mr. Pemberton, and accepted the steaming tea proffered by Mrs. Bidgood, though Mr. Pemberton winked and nudged and said he was very welcome to something a little stronger if he was so disposed. The constable smiled, and toasted his legs in front of the fire. He had returned, he explained, to inform them of developments. What they'd found out, he said, agreed substantially with the information given by yonder lads. The man felled by Mr. Pemberton's umbrella was the quiet, cold man Laurie and Frank had overheard. A very nasty piece of goods, added the constable with some satisfaction. The man caught by Laurie and Frank was the handsome young man sent to incriminate Emmy. Everyone looked toward Emmy at this, and she blushed and frowned and repeated for the third time the story of her relations with that young man. She *had* been flattered when he took notice of her, but when she spent her half-day with him she soon saw what an empty, vain thing he was, and told him not to call again, but he'd laughed, and said she was a tease, and *wouldn't* be told! Everyone ummed and nodded, and Mrs. Bidgood patted Emmy's hand comfortingly, and gave it as her opinion that young devils like that were all chirp and cheek.

Questing, apparently, had denied everything—had even tried to say he'd heard a noise downstairs, had come to investigate, and was actually running for a constable when overcome. They all had a good laugh at this. Most important of all, though, was the fact that they'd got the name and whereabouts of the "principal" referred to by the soft-voiced man when the boys had first got wind of the affair on Christmas Eve. The good-looking young man had yielded this, knowing he was in very deep, and hoping to gain clemency by cooperating with the police. Some top men were even then on the way to arrest this "principal," an evil and ruthless man long known to be a force in London crime, though too clever to be caught —till now.

After his third cup of tea the constable announced that he was much obliged, he was sure, but business was business and he must be on his way. Laurie accompanied him to the front door, and watched him disappear behind the curtain of rain. After that he stood there half hypnotized by the dreary gray downpour. It was like the last scene of a play or the last chapter of a book, he thought—the explanations, the gaps filled in, the ends tied up. Suddenly he felt very tired and flat—uneasy, too. He'd been in London such a long time, and it was so cold and dark. What sort of a day was it going to be in Sydney? He imagined a bright blue day with the harbor sparkling, and wondered whether he could persuade his mother to take him to Balmoral Beach. Sun biting into his skin, that's what he craved, and the laughter of people with full stomachs and with houses to go home to. He shivered and stepped back into the hall, thinking what a short time perfect happiness lasts, for they *had* been perfectly happy when they'd steamed noisily and boastfully into the house, the glorious Victors who would soon be the Warm and the Fed as well. He sighed and felt pleased with his thought, which seemed to him to be very deep and grand and sad.

Back in the drawing room, he found Frank recounting, apparently at Mr. Pemberton's insistence, the story of his trek to London, and all that had befallen him since. Mr. Pemberton was quite awed.

". . . and so you sang for your supper and then you . . . and with a bad foot, too, or did you say a bad back? Jove, I'd like my son to hear this. A good lad, a very good lad, but I'm afraid his mother coddles him rather, *and* his aunts. I daresay even I, at times, may have been a bit . . . but under a boat, you say, sleeping under a boat? Of all the. . . . What spirit! And learning to read like that. See here, you're going to tell all this to Francis, I don't care what they say!" The gleam in Mr. Pemberton's eye was enough to quell any number of brothers-in-law, if he could only keep it there long enough.

Laurie fidgeted, shifted his weight from foot to foot, yawned, and finally interrupted. "I think I'd better go now," he said, with a long, meaningful look at Frank.

140

"Oh, must you?" said Mr. Pemberton, who had never enjoyed a night so much, and didn't want it to end.

"Yes, really. My family will be wondering where I am," replied Laurie, hoping very much that his family, though not yet born, was sleeping peacefully.

"Well, if you must," sighed Mr. Pemberton, disappointed. "It is a long way to Clerkenwell, I suppose."

"Clerkenwell?" repeated Laurie blankly, so tired he'd forgotten his own lie.

"Now there's a funny thing," said Frank, stepping in smoothly to cover Laurie's lapse. "I didn't know you lived in Clerkenwell, Laurie. I had it in my head that it was, let me think—began with an S, I think—Stepney? It just shows, don't it? I mean, doesn't it?" He winked at Laurie and smiled. His smile was one of the things Laurie liked best about him, and he would have liked to reply in kind, but Mr. Pemberton was looking at him, so he could only direct a little smirk of amusement and thanks toward Frank.

"I'll see myself out, Mr. Pemberton. Thanks for the food and everything—it's been great. No, it's quite OK—all right, I mean—I know the way. Well," he paused at the door, "good-bye, Mr. Pemberton. See you, Frank."

"See you," replied Frank, with another big smile, for he knew perfectly well that this was a twentieth-century expression. Laurie had taught him any number of them.

141

11

L aurie was to remember those last smiles and be grateful that they parted on that note, for he never saw Frank again. Whether his long stay had in fact exhausted the magic, or whether its purpose was accomplished when Frank learned to read and write, or when the burglary had been averted, there was no way of knowing. If the latter, then it seemed pretty silly that centuries had been shaken and lives turned upside down simply to preserve Grandfather Pemberton's clock and other articles no doubt well insured, and in any case owned by a man well able to afford replacements. But perhaps this wasn't it, perhaps nothing that Laurie could think of was "it"— perhaps magic needs no reason.

After a week of waiting and expecting to go back, all the time thinking of more things he wanted to say to Frank, Laurie grew really worried, and began to

142

spend so much time in and on the bed that his parents became concerned about him again. More time went by, and there was the new school to be faced, ordeal enough without aching for a lost friend as well. Especially hard was the fact that this misery had to be carried around inside him all the time, and never let out, except with Clare, who patiently endured all his anxiety for Frank's welfare, and many rambling and repetitive tales of London and London life.

First term went on. Laurie settled down at school and made a few friends, and Rosie decided she quite liked North Sydney. All in all, normality. Then, crashing down, another shock. Clare came in after school one day with the important air of someone with something to communicate. After she'd been maddeningly mysterious for ten minutes or so, Laurie adjourned to the apricot tree, where he hoped she'd open up if she was going to. She did.

It seemed her class was doing a project on the history of the North Sydney area. Her particular assignment was to interview three long-time residents, with family roots going back to the early days of settlement. She'd done two already. One was with an old gentleman of ninety-three from whom she hadn't been able to glean much, apart from his fiercely-held conviction that the Harbour Bridge was going to collapse in 1982. This was supported by incontrovertible proof in the form of pages of calculations conforming to no known mathematical laws, which "They" had been refusing

143

to publish for years. The second was with an elderly and rather deaf lady who chiefly remembered when ladies *had* been ladies, and who thought North Sydney sadly gone down nowadays.

"So?" said Laurie, bored and irritated, because he knew there must be more, and why wouldn't she get to it.

"The third one I haven't seen yet. I thought you might like to come."

"Why?"

"Because," said Clare, slowly and exultingly (here we go thought Laurie wearily), "his name is KILDER-BEE, that's why."

Laurie tried to be calm as he stood outside Mr. Kilderbee's door with Clare, but excitement kept stirring up inside him, however hard he tried to dampen it and however often he told himself it must be the merest coincidence.

Mr. Kilderbee, when he opened the door, proved disappointing. Here was no image of Frank, but a pleasant-looking man of average height and a little more than average weight—a nice, curly-haired dumpling of a man.

"Oh, you must be the young lady who wrote. And a young gentleman, too? I hadn't realized . . . Clare, isn't it? And you're . . . ?"

They introduced themselves while he fussed around and made them comfortable in the friendliest manner. Two lovely, placid cats eyed them sleepily from a shabby chair in which they were curled together, and a large dog opened one eye and thumped his feathery tail on the floor two or three times as his contribution to the welcome.

"Don't mind them, they're tired," said Mr. Kilderbee. "We've been working in the garden all day."

It sounded as though cats, dog, and man had all been working, and mad visions of cats wielding spades and dogs pulling weeds and hosing flowers were arranging themselves in Laurie's head, when his eye lighted on something that emptied his mind of every thought but one, and that one was that either he was looking at Grandfather Pemberton's clock or he was a Dutchman!

It was just as well Clare had the interview well in hand, for Laurie was so totally disabled by his discovery that he sat silent and gaping for so long that Mr. Kilderbee started darting curious glances toward him.

When the first shock receded and Laurie came to, as it were, it was to hear Mr. Kilderbee declaring proudly that yes, his family *had* been connected with the North Sydney area for a long time. His great-grandfather had built this very house—Sydney sandstone, marvelous wasn't it, it would last forever—in 1878, the year of his marriage.

145

"What was his name?" Laurie interjected, so suddenly, and in such a strangled, croaky voice, that Mr. Kilderbee almost jumped in his chair.

"His name was Francis Kilderbee. There's been a Francis in the family ever since—in my case it comes second, though. I'm Robert Francis."

"And he came from London?" pursued Laurie, not daring to meet Clare's glance, which he knew was fixed on him.

"Did I mention that in my letter? Good gracious! Yes, he came from London. So did his wife, but he met her here, not there."

"And what did he do?" The questions came relentlessly, but Mr. Kilderbee, who was a kindly soul, was relieved to find that Laurie *could* talk after all, and besides, he enjoyed talking about his family.

"He was a vet. That is, I don't know whether he had any formal qualifications, but he was very fond of animals and apparently looked after everyone's horses and poultry and cats and dogs for miles around, and did very well. He could easily have had professional training, now I think of it, for he was well educated."

"*Was* he?" Laurie seized on this as being tremendously important. (My goodness, how youngsters throw themselves into their school work these days, thought poor, innocent Mr. Kilderbee.)

"Yes, indeed. And that's an interesting story in itself. . . ." Mr. Kilderbee crossed his legs and settled back for a nice chat, till he recalled the purpose of

146

the interview. ". . . But perhaps it's not relevant, as it has nothing to do with North Sydney."

"What hasn't? His education? Please tell us. It's very interesting, and, well, it's all background material, isn't it? I mean, he *was* a pioneer."

Well pleased, and thinking the younger generation much underrated if these were typical specimens, Mr. Kilderbee expanded.

"Well, you see, my great-grandfather began life much more humbly than he ended it. His own father was a drunkard, from whom he ran away, to scrape a living for himself in London—only a lad, mind—working as a crossing sweeper." He paused. "You probably don't know what a crossing sweeper is."

Wouldn't he have been astonished to learn that his listeners could have answered, "Oh yes, we've swept a few crossings ourselves!" Instead, they just nodded, not trusting themselves to speak.

"You do? My goodness! And they say children don't learn anything these days!" Much impressed, Mr. Kilderbee continued. "Well, somehow—we don't know just how it was—old Francis attracted the attention of a wealthy man called Pemberton. We know the Pembertons lived in the same street, or was it a square, that my great-grandfather regularly swept, so probably they met right there in the street. Now this Mr. Pemberton had a son, also called Francis—odd, isn't it?—and this son was rather delicate and spoiled—a milksop and mummy's boy, in fact. Now, Mr. Pemberton got it into his head that young Master Francis needed

147

toughening up, and for whatever reason, decided the crossing sweeper was just the lad to do it! He must have been something of an eccentric, for you may not know—but then, perhaps you do—that in those days it would have seemed the worst kind of folly for someone of his class to take up a member of what they called the 'lower orders' like that. Am I boring you? No, I see I'm not? Well, Mr. Pemberton *did* strike opposition. His wife was dead against it, and so was her family, who were people of some importance, I believe. But Mr. Pemberton wouldn't be shifted, and brought my great-grandfather right into the house. Would you like some tea?"

It took Laurie and Clare a moment to realize they were being questioned. They thought they'd better say yes, because Mr. Kilderbee obviously fancied a little something himself, and they wanted to keep him as contented and chatty as possible. So the story was interrupted for ten minutes, and resumed to the accompaniment of tea and apple pie and ginger biscuits.

"Where was I? Oh, I know. Well, young Master Francis himself ended all dispute, by taking to young Frank to such an extent that he declared that if they sent him away he'd never forgive them, and promptly got asthma at the very thought. So that was that. And as it happened, Mrs. Pemberton soon came round when she got to know Frank, and they were all very happy together—though I understand things were never the same with her family again. More tea?"

148

"No, thank you," both replied, and Laurie added, "So the Pembertons educated him, did they?"

"Yes. That's what I started out to tell you, isn't it? Has it really taken me so long to get there? Yes, he was educated with the young master. Frank had taught himself to read and write somehow or other, and he must have been exceedingly bright, for he made great strides. He and Master Francis were like brothers—Francis came to Australia to visit him a few years after he came out."

"When did he—Frank—come?"

"1872. He was twenty-two. The Pembertons were distracted at the idea of losing him, but he had it firmly in his head that he was going to Australia. Goodness knows why, what could he have know about the place? Yet he must have had his reasons—he knew just what part he meant to come to. Intriguing, isn't it? Wait a bit though, I've got something inside that may interest you."

He left the room and, for the first time, Laurie and Clare were able to exchange the looks and words and thoughts that had been bubbling inside them since the interview began. Laurie was in such a state that his pent-up feelings could only be relieved by striding up and down the room waving his arms wildly, to the mild alarm of the cats and the pleased attention of the dog, who watched closely, trying to work out what sort of game this was.

Mr. Kilderbee returned clutching a handful of old

books and papers and folders, and mumbling about something's being here somewhere. Then, with a "Ha!" of triumph he drew forth a photo, and handed it to Laurie.

"There! What do you think of that?"

The photo, remarkably clear for its age, showed a young man standing in an easy attitude, hand on hip. He was tall and lean, with laughing eyes and a frank, straight look about him that must have made just about anyone like him at sight. Frank, of course. He was smiling down at a dark spaniel that gazed back adoringly.

"Aged twenty-six," said Mr. Kilderbee. "A few years before his marriage."

It made Laurie feel distinctly queer to look at it. Less than two months before, he'd been talking to this man—only then the man had been a boy. He felt very young and left behind, as though Frank had taken some unfair advantage of him and magically shot ahead to adulthood. Which was silly, he knew, because Frank was not ahead of but far, far behind him. And that brought up another question, one that would have to be asked, because he never had heard from Somerset House.

"When . . . when did he die?"

"Oh, I know that. 1918. It's stayed in my mind because I remember my grandfather saying he was always thankful that his father had lived to see peace return."

Sixty-eight, calculated Laurie, and absently turned

the photo over. There, in faded script, were the words "Rosie and I, Lavender Bay, 1876." He passed it to Clare, who read it and looked as though she was going to cry; and Laurie didn't blame her one bit.

Recovering herself, Clare eyed the heap of papers and books and albums that Mr. Kilderbee had brought in, and had one of her ideas.

"Your great-grandfather sounds so interesting that I think I'd like to do my whole project on him. Only," she continued slowly, "I don't suppose there's enough information." She finished on a note of wistful regret, with the tiniest hint of question in her voice. Fishing, definitely fishing, thought Laurie, and waited to see if she would get a bite.

"*Loads!* Really, there's loads of stuff," exclaimed Mr. Kilderbee, rising enthusiastically to the bait. Bless the man, thought Laurie, and bless Clare, too, forgiving her again for all the times she'd driven him to distraction.

So the two of them went to work, and Mr. Kilderbee hadn't exaggerated—there *was* loads of stuff. Suppose Frank had left it for them, in case they should ever be on his tracks? The trail was such an easy one that at times they were convinced that this was not just a nice idea but plain truth. There were diaries and drawings and account books and letters and photos and all kinds of things like that. The most thrilling discovery was a crumpled and blurred photo that Clare found among some old postcards. At the first sight of it, she became so pink and white and hot and cold and pleased

152

and solemn that Laurie thought she'd taken leave of her senses—till he looked, too. It showed Frank and Clare, sitting together in front of a homemade back-cloth depicting some swag drapes, a curving staircase that would have tipped off anyone who tried to climb it, and a pair of columns that rivaled the leaning tower of Pisa for angle. Frank was trying to swagger but was half awed by the occasion, and Clare looked the complete Victorian young lady. It was a wonderful find.

Before long they knew as much as it was possible to know of Frank's life—his coming to Australia; the building of the house in which they worked (for Mr. Kilderbee, though he gave them free access to it, would not let them take the material away); his courtship of Judith, a music teacher, and his marriage in nearby St. Thomas's church; his joy in his family of two boys and a girl. Here came another discovery—the second son was called Laurence, the daughter Judith Clare. This was even better evidence than that provided by Rosie the dog that Frank had not forgotten, and it touched them. Did he ever tell his wife? They would love to have known, but that was one question their research couldn't answer.

Frank wrote quite a bit about his "patients" and his own pets in his diaries, and these were the parts Laurie liked best. They were full of concern for the animals when they were sick, and could be very funny about them when they were well. Rosie, it seemed, was not terribly bright, a foolish but loving animal. Pete, who followed her, was her exact opposite—a genius of a dog, whom it was impossible to deceive. "He quite frightens us," wrote Frank, "and after a very unequal struggle I, for one, have decided to give him best. I'll never even try to leave home without him again. It can't be done, and I may as well give in gracefully."

There was an untitled drawing of a bright-eyed, prick-eared dog that Laurie decided must be Pete, and must be by Frank himself. It brought back vivid memories of a poor little drawing on a torn scrap of paper that he'd seen decorating Frank's room in Catherine Wheel Alley.

Laurie had good reason to be proud of his pupil, for Frank wrote well, in a light, easy style. Possibly he took more pleasure in writing than the average person because he'd come by the skill so late. Certainly, sheer enjoyment in the power of writing things down shone through every page; and every so often, some word or phrase would leap out at Laurie, confirming him in his conviction that Frank had written with the idea that he might see it one day. It must have seemed a remote possibility, but a possibility just the same, and worth providing for. For instance, in one place he mentioned having just had to boat to "town" on business, and then speculated on the possibility of a bridge being built across the harbor one day, "which would be very convenient, but, things being what they are, it will probably be 1932 or so before it's done, rather too late to benefit me." If *that* wasn't a private, tongue-in-cheek joke with Laurie, the only person who could ever know that he hadn't just pulled the date out of a hat, then Laurie didn't know what was.

When the project was finished they left it with Mr. Kilderbee, thinking it only right that he should see it first. Some compliment they expected, because they knew it was good, but on their return several days later Mr. Kilderbee overwhelmed them with his amazement and praise.

"I honestly don't know how you did it. One would almost think you'd been there! I'm overcome, really I am. I can't wait for you to grow up and write a whole book about the old boy. I always thought I would, but you'd obviously do it so much better. Would you like some tea?"

He'd invented and baked a new cake to celebrate the occasion, from an unusual assortment of ingredients including apple cider and cherries, and they had fun inventing a name for it while they ate and drank, all very pleased with themselves and each other.

The job was done, but there was no sadness in the occasion, because the friendship established with Mr. Kilderbee was off to a good start, and seemed likely to continue. He was a nice man, and although he didn't look like Frank (except, Laurie had decided, around the eyes) nearness to him was as near to Frank as it was possible to get now.

Bob—as he now insisted they call him—was just showing them out the front door when he slapped his forehead and hurried back inside, muttering something about forgetting his head if it wasn't stuck on. Laurie and Clare stood by the door with the dog and the cats, wondering, not very concernedly, what had been forgotten. On his return, Mr. Kilderbee held something in each hand.

"Here," he said, "I want you to have these," and handed each of them a heavy mug. "I don't know their provenance," he hurried on, as if to forestall their thanks, "but by the look of the old queen there, they must have belonged to my great-grandfather himself. I feel you deserve them, after all your interest and trouble."

The identical mugs showed a portrait of Queen Victoria in early middle age, unamused as ever. A pair of Union Jacks was crossed behind her, and she was surrounded by a wreath of stiff flowers. On the back of the mug was the Prince of Wales, in much less pomp and looking a bit huffy about it. Beautiful they were not, but they *were* old, and it was most generous of Mr. Kilderbee—Bob—to give them away like that. Not that it was his generosity that silenced Laurie. What did was the fact that the mug was now his indeed, for it was his twice over. Bob gave it to him now—but Frank had given it to him first, one hundred and sixteen years before. It was the one he'd tried to bring home and couldn't, and he well remembered Frank's disappointment when both mugs—his and Clare's—had to be returned. "All right, but remember it's still yours," he had said, and Laurie had made a point of drinking out of it on the few occasions when he'd been in Frank's room. How pleased he would be to know that his gift had come home at last—and through the hand of his own great-grandson! If only it were possible to go back to Cavendish Square one more time to tell him. How they would laugh!

Or would they laugh? It was queer—it had all been queer, really—and now, to end it, this mysterious reaching out of friend to friend across the years. He remembered that Clare didn't yet know just what it was she was thanking Bob for so politely, and couldn't wait to tell her.